FIRE FROM THE HEIGHTS

BOOK ONE

Tishbe in Gilead was an austere place. One or two of its inhabitants would perhaps claim that they made an adequate living; most would say that they clung to life, as a juniper clung to its rock-shelf in the surrounding crags. Most of their homes clustered at the wide entrance to the wadi that ran, northwesterly, into the high and almost wholly barren hills. Further out into the plain, the more temporary encampments housed the nomadic peoples of the wilderness and desert, some with their small flocks of sheep, the poorer sort herding a few goats. These were sharper-featured, with the high cheekbones and narrow foreheads which seemed to set them apart from their kin in the permanent settlement and gave them an affinity with their distant cousins of the desert oases. In its humbly miniature way, Tishbe was as much like a staging-post as a permanent agricultural settlement.

The colours were sharp in the evening sunlight; the highest crags of the wadi, their brown sandstone black as basalt in the westering light, were threaded in their lower slopes with lines of green, where the small springs allowed a little grass to maintain its hold. In the clefts above these runnels, thorn and occasional junipers promised a deeper soil in which an acacia sometimes bloomed but never reached more than the twisted height of a bush.

At the entrance to one of the wider openings in the wadi cliffs a rather more comfortable house than the average had been built of dressed blocks from the sandstone cliffs. A small fire – more for visual comfort than warmth – crackled in the centre of the courtyard; before it were seated, on roughly hewn logs, a man in his full vigour and strength and a boy of about fifteen years. They held the silence of an inconclusive argument, a controlled pleading in the man's eyes, a stubbornly-set mouth promising no yielding on the boy's part.

"I ask you for no more than a year or two's shepherding until Reuven can take over the flocks in the upper reaches. He isn't yet ready for the long days alone in those waste places and doesn't yet know either the scattered pastures or the length of time a flock can graze without destroying its future store of food. Take him for just one more early spring before the lambing."

It was clearly a painful and unusual discipline, this father's pleading, and he groped for a way to penetrate his son's silence.

"If Tishbe wearies you, take Reuven and cross the hills to the Brook Kerith. I have hoped for some seasons to be able to beg a strip of richer pasture from my cousin Jacob, where the lambs can be fattened in the early spring. You would be away for no more than five or perhaps six days and I could just manage the flocks for that brief time."

"Kerith! our neighbouring stream!" The boy Elijah was conceding nothing to his father's plea but generations of paternal authority forced him to an explanation.

"Since I became a man" – the wry smile of early adolescence invited his father's understanding – "I have been driven in mind beyond Tishbe. It is like a voice

10

Moelwyn Merchant was born in Port Talbot in 1913 and educated in University College, Cardiff where he read Honours degrees in English and History. He become a Reader in the University of Wales, Professor of English in the University of Exeter and Willett Professor in the University of Chicago.

He was Canon and Chancellor of Salisbury Cathedral and then returned to Wales to become Vicar of Llanddewibrefi. He now lives in Leamington Spa.

Apart from many works of academic criticism, he has published three books of poetry and in 1987 published *Jeshua,* a novel based on the life of Christ. He is a fellow of the Royal Society of Literature.

Starting at the age of fifty-four to be a sculptor, he has had some thirty one-man shows and shared three exhibitions with his friend Josef Herman, who has designed and drawn the book cover.

Princeton Theological Monograph Series

Dikran Y. Hadidian

General Editor

27

FIRE FROM THE HEIGHTS

by the same author

Breaking the Code (*Poetry*)
No Dark Glass (*Poetry*)
Confrontation of Angels (*Poetry*)
Jeshua (*Novel*)

FIRE FROM THE HEIGHTS

Moelwyn Merchant

PICKWICK PUBLICATIONS
ALLISON PARK, PENNSYLVANIA

Copyright © Moelwyn Merchant 1987

First published in Great Britain 1987
    by Christopher Davies (Publishers) Ltd.
        P.O. Box 403, Sketty
        Swansea, SA2 9BE

First published in the United States of America   1991
    by Pickwick Publications
        4137 Timberlane Drive
        Allison Park, PA 15101

Library of Congress Cataloging-in-Publication Data

Merchant, W. Moelwyn (William Moelwyn), 1913-
    Fire from the heights / Moelwyn Merchant
       p.   cm. -- (Princeton theological monograph series ; 27)
    ISBN 1-55635-011-2
    1. Elijah (Biblical prophet)--Fiction. 2. Bible. O.T.--History
of Biblical events--Fiction. I. Title. II. Series.
PR6063.E72F57   1991
823'.914--dc20

                             91-8325
                             CIP

in the depth of my hearing, a voice with no words, no message but it urges me to some action, some movement away from this safe place. I love Tishbe as I love you, my family. You tell me that I'm skilled with the flocks, that they trust me. But when I speak, in those desolate places, with Reuven, as we prepare for the night's rest, I know that I am different. He is clever, has words beyond mine; he would be both a shepherd and a rabbi in any place like ours – or much larger. But he's gentle also. He has never really understood me when I speak of my 'voice.' His heart is contented; he understands what our royal singer meant by 'green pastures' and 'still waters.' I don't think I shall ever know that stillness."

Spring was late that year and the harsh winter had made shepherding harder than usual. The small flocks – rarely more than ten or twelve – had been kept to the lower slopes and even then, at the evening gather to the folds, they had to be given a handful or two of the dried fodder, so carefully gathered and stored at the end of the previous year.

And some of the hardier and venturesome young men had disturbing word to say at the evening fire, of a lean predator from the upper mountain – one said he was sure that it was a young leopard – who threatened any wanderer from the flock. Twice, so he said, only the most threatening shouts from him had driven the creature off, while he gathered the few sheep that he tended, some of them near the yeaning and unfit for threats.

Elijah listened without comment and the next day at dawn set out alone, with two agile young sheep, as if to test them on the steeper slopes. He had chosen his favourite staff, a long ash-plant, widely curved at one end and iron-shod at the other. If leopard there was to be encountered he knew where it might be found; he

11

felt certain that his brisk young beasts would be a tempting but not too vulnerable decoy and made as fast as possible for the upper hills.

He avoided the scree slopes – footing would be too precarious – and went to a defile where overhanging ledges had shown him in past years that they gave shelter to such a creature as he now hunted. He had not allowed the two sheep to graze as they made their way upward but drove them away from any pasture and on to the bare rock paths.

At a sharp curve in the climb and a few yards from a ledge which stretched over the path, twice a man's height above him, he held his sheep at his side and stood poised, waiting for their impatient bleat as they demanded fodder. The younger and stronger – a ram just beginning to feel its male strength – bleated loudly and was then held silent by the crook of Elijah's staff. He listened and, as he had hoped, there was a rustle in the loose stones of the ledge above and the throaty rumble of a hunting beast.

Elijah stood away from the ram, releasing it from the crook. Its bleat brought a clumsier stirring on the ledge above and, with one swift look, the leopard jumped for its prey. Elijah stood aside from the path of its leap and held the iron tip of the staff ready for its plunge. When the leopard was within half the distance from the ledge, Elijah thrust with what was now a spear, the weight and falling leap of the leopard carrying it so violently on to the point that the staff snapped as it pierced deep into the leopard's throat.

The death of young lambs taught every shepherd at springtime the unhappy skills of flaying. The leopard was just dead when Elijah swiftly began to remove its pelt and, leaving the carcase to the eagle which already circled above him, made his way to the village below.

"There is a meeting of instincts here, Elijah, and they lay a choice before you. These last years have seen you grow to full manhood but we still speak of 'the day of the leopard' and indeed many of our kin think of you as 'Tishbe's mighty hunter'! But I have greater reason for pride. I asked you for a few years to allow Reuven to grow to your strength and skills before you made your decision. This you have done and I owe you now your choice.

"These instincts – the instincts of our people – clash within you, perhaps more violently in you than in most of your kin. The first is the impulse of the wanderer, the traveller in the waste, the distant places. The other is the instinct for home, the sojourner, the builder of villages, towns and cities. And for some people they tear and tug at the soul. Our father Abraham was such a man. A citizen of a noble city – for Ur of the Chaldeans was a city notable even among the richest in the Land of the Rivers. Abraham lived with honour and great wealth – flocks and possessions beyond numbering – and no man in his land had greater reason to be content with his lot. And he was content, for many years. Then came the stirring in the blood, that instinct which drives men over the waste places, even – and this has always confounded me – over the trackless seas. With his kin, his flocks and herds, he left the secure city, its comfort and its honour, and went westward. On that march there seemed nothing but desert before them and I have often thought of the sombre evening camp-fires, the oases left behind them, as they debated the madness of the way ahead. But there was no debate in Abraham's mind. Without a word, each night was but a preparation for the morning and the striking of camp, and the trek, ever westward towards the setting sun."

Judah's voice had itself taken on a sombre note as he explored the light in his son's eyes. Elijah knew the

Abraham story as clearly as his father but this choice at the heart of the story had never before been clear to him.

"And he came to a city, and settled from his wanderings?"

Reluctantly Elijah allowed the unlikely possibility to grow to an expressed idea.

"No; that was Lot's part. The cities of the plain, the comfort of their houses, the riches of their trade, these held Lot in their grasp but not Abraham! He chose still, even within the bounds of the land which God had given him, the open uplands, the wild grazing-places, the tracks from well to well. His paths were still the water-courses, his ways the wanderings of his flocks."

Elijah knew that he was listening to words and tones that were as rare in his father's voice as they were unfamiliar to him. His father, born in Tishbe and son to a prosperous shepherd of Tishbe, had never for more than a few days moved from the confined horizons of its hills and wadis. Now Elijah heard tones, wholly unexpected but carrying in their yearnings, inadmissible until now, a power to which he wholly responded.

"What is my choice, then?" It was a question to which any answer would seem confounding. To accept Tishbe as his 'city of the plain', to make it a dwelling-place, with all that that meant of family, home, labour and wealth; or to strike out, eastward into the desert or westward to the Jordan and beyond?

His father's eyes had lost their questing and he now waited patiently for the answer.

"I cannot say! My 'Voice' says 'Go; make your way into the open places, even the desert' and my heart says 'Stay! This is home and kin.'"

"And your 'Voice'; what else does it say beyond 'Go!'? Has it words to declare? You can't, a skilled shepherd,

14

be merely the servant of your feet, a mere wanderer of the earth! Has it anything more for you to do and say?"

"That I can learn only on the way. I have no mind to reason and argue like Reuven's. I am no rabbi! I barely know the roads followed by Joseph, the bitter toil of Moses from Sinai, the blood and toil of Joshua – but I have my 'voice' and I trust in him. I can't say more, father; the choice is not yet forced on me."

To someone from the cities, the senses of these dwellers at the desert fringes would have seemed almost atrophied. The ways and the urgencies of life itself, food and the propagation of family would seem simple, even primitive. Food was rarely more than mere sustenance; even Passover chewed with more awareness of the bitter herb, the unleavened bread, than the succulence of roast in the mouth. Children were a blessing and a momentary joy but love was sparing at their begetting and one child beyond the yield of their field or flock could be a tragedy.

The weeks had not resolved Elijah's mind. Few of the consequences of either choice were clear to him as facts, concrete decisions to be weighed. Work was the immediate choice and he thrust himself into more than his customary daily labour.

It was late afternoon in the season of lambing. The flocks had been more than usually restless and had needed great vigilance as they were brought to the lower enclosures, the ewes kept in such comfort as was possible. Elijah sat on a large boulder beneath a fig-tree at the village entrance and drowsed away some of the day's fatigue in the early evening sun. He was beyond thought, as his limbs relaxed from the day's work and after a while of resting, his eyes turned to the shadows of the desert fringe.

"My real home, Elijah."

15

He looked up, startled by the unexpected voice and saw Miriam, the orphan from the desert ways, who had been taken to their home by his cousins in the village. It had been a strange chance. Three or four sheep had wandered from the flock, and, perhaps scenting water on the light breeze, perhaps the illusion of an oasis, had moved into the hopelessness of the desert. The shepherd following them had gone much further than his first intention and, gathering them in, had decided on a slight circuit homewards, to take in a well before the night journey. The water there was usually brackish but some grassy growth and the shelter of a few shrubs promised rest before the return. As he approached the place he heard the thin cry as of a new-born lamb and found beneath one of the shrubs a huddled infant, lost from its nomadic family. Parched and starving, nothing could be done for it but to carry it as gently as could be to his home in Tishbe.

With their care the child prospered and grew to be Miriam, the loved foundling whose eyes were frequently turned to the desert.

"My real home, Elijah."

His eyes followed the direction of her gaze and his thoughts followed hers, to be united with his father's words as he spoke of wilderness and city and the parting of ways. Her voice again interrupted his thinking and he was startled to find her echoing matters in his mind that he had not expressed.

"You will be leaving us, Elijah, perhaps for always, and we shall miss you very sorely."

There was solemnity in the depths of her eyes and she spoke, not in the light tones of a young woman's conversation but with a measured sureness like the beginnings of prophecy.

"And you will not marry?" As she spoke he looked more intently at her. Until now she had been accepted as a child is accepted, without calculation. She had been Miriam from the desert ways saved from death by mere chance. Now, with word of marriage, he looked at her with unaccustomed eyes. She was comely, fair-skinned and with eyes of unusual lightness of colour, honey-coloured rather than the black-brown of his cousins. Her hair was fine in texture and was drawn smoothly across her shoulders, framing the long oval of her face.

He looked and saw her for the first time as warmly desirable and, as he looked, was shocked to find in himself no trace of desire. It was not as though she were sisterly, not as though she was already betrothed. His instinct told him that were he to show desire, her eyes would respond, warm with the import of her question, 'You will not marry?' In that moment he knew that a wholly unconscious decision had already been made for him; he would never marry, never know the parted consciousness, the sharing of love.

He smiled at her and raising his hand to hers, drew her down to sit at his side.

"What do you remember of your life before Tishbe? – for you were little more than a helpless infant!"

"I know only that I was happy. There was always someone or some creature to carry me and after days of hot desert, the sand in my mouth and my eyes, an oasis camp was like a glimpse of heaven! And there were the sweet fruits to go with the dry, hard bread, dates plump from the palm and pomegranates bursting their pulp into my mouth. I seem to remember few smiles around me but those strong, tired faces never frowned, were never angry but were patient even with a fretful child!"

Elijah had never used words like this even to himself; his parents were his parents, Reuven was Reuven, his cousins and friends were unanalysed cousins and friends. Here was a new world of the mind. In Miriam's quiet

17

gaze he knew that he and all men were there to be understood, measured, perhaps even judged?

There was a long silence between them as the shadows spread and the breeze of evening raised miniature eddies in the sand at their feet. Then the quiet voice went on:

"Days in the open desert would heal the scars of your questioning Elijah. You can't travel far to the east without finding an oasis, and where there's an oasis you will surely find my kin. They will have much to tell you."

He drew her to her feet and in silence they went to their homes.

Due east it had been. Tamarisk, juniper and the thorn of the wilderness-fringe had given way to true desert, gold and gravelly or the fine silver of dried watercourses. After many days in which hunger could be partly satisfied but thirst became intolerable, he reached an oasis, larger than any he had seen before. There was a well, protected by a wall and wooden covering, and a spring which created a miniature pond fringed with rushes and stunted papyrus, and beyond its margin a pasturage that he coveted for his Tishbe flock. But he was alone there and having picked carefully a handful of the succulent dates, he sat by the palm for his evening meal. The dates surprised him; they were twice as large as any he had known at home and much less sweet, and he supposed that in this more friendly soil the sun had not reduced the fruit to their half-dried concentration of sweetness. He carefully peeled the upper half of a pomegranate and after sucking out all the pulp, used the cupped lower half of the rind, like a gourd, to give himself a drink from the spring. Then the dreamless sleep of fatigue and the desert stillness.

Two days passed in almost thoughtless solitude. If

there were thoughts, they were no more than a consciousness of waiting, without expectation or definition but with patience. Then on the third evening there was the sound of the shuffling gait of camels, just five of them and a small company of men and women with three children poised before them on the saddles.

They accepted Elijah as though he were an expected visitor and, as night fell, there was a frugal meal of barley-cakes, cheese – rather bitter, as of mare's milk – some raisins and figs, and with water to drink.

"Tomorrow we feast." Elijah must have shown his disbelief, for, with no more than a smile, they prepared him a bed of small boughs covered by a saddle-blanket.

The following morning they explained their promise of the previous evening that today they would feast.

"We shall be glad of your help. On our way we saw ahead of us a flight of quail. It can be no more than an hour's journey, for they will surely alight at the grassy verge of a small water-hole which we must reach before them." When they came to the water-hole they spread over it and the surrounding grass a fine-meshed net and then withdrew to a hollow in the hilly sand to await the flight. It came swiftly in and made for the customary feeding-ground. The men rose, with cries and clapped hands and in a flurry of flight most of the quails made away. But some twenty were caught in the meshes and were deftly taken loose.

"We need no more than twelve," they said and allowed the others to fly away. Back at the encampment the quails were quickly feathered and cleaned, the fire was built to a roasting heat and the birds, spitted three to a peeled branch, were held before the fire and quickly cooked. It was indeed a feast and Elijah felt wholly adopted by the company.

With no embarrassing curiosity, it was clear that the nomadic group would be happy to understand his

19

solitary appearance among them. Elijah was clearly learning for himself, and gradually, as he spoke, he cleared his mind.

"I am of Tishbe, a shepherd and the son of a shepherd. With my sheep in the high pastures I am at rest, content with the work I do, seeking fodder, protecting the weaker ewes, the joy in life and increase at lambing and sometimes the passing sorrows, a ram lost to a jackal as he tries to protect his strays. It fills me to the driving out of thought. But there is the quiet safety of the fold, the flock gathered and the hurdle set; when I rest there across the entrance and the folds of my mantle sit comfortably beneath shoulder and thigh, then thinking floods back again."

There was a smiling assent from the older men in the company and they nodded, remembering their night-thoughts.

"Does Jahweh demand no more than shepherding? Am I to know no more than Tishbe, its few springs and the harsh rocks? These are the questions that my 'Voice' pours into my mind."

"Your voice?" It was scarcely a question but the eyes of the oldest among his hosts seemed almost to anticipate Elijah's reply.

"It is my 'Voice', speaks to me alone and yet – it is not my voice; I don't speak the words, for they come, like an echo in the high passes. It says little. Often it's no more than my name: 'Elijah, Elijah' it says and the single name is like a command, that I go out to meet the 'Voice', to follow its urgency."

The women had withdrawn to see to their tired children and there were just five of them about the fire, four of the wandering tribesmen and Elijah, struggling to make himself understood, to make his words sound rational.

"God speaks with many voices. We have a custom, private to ourselves: on days of especial calm, the dew not yet rising to the sun's warmth, we set out before we have said all the morning psalms." He smiled as Elijah showed his surprise which seemed to be tinged with reproof.

"Those are the mornings when the psalms of our father David have reached 'the great Hallel' and the words of joy sound like a marching-song as we sing them aloud in the morning stillness. That is the moment when Adonai speaks to me, His words of quiet wisdom."

Elijah knew that here was one of the answers and at the breaking of camp the following morning, he joined them for their first day's journey from the oasis, insisting that he needed no mount but would trot along on foot. He quickly fell into the rhythm of the journey and when, by evening, they reached a shallow valley northeast of Tishbe, he seemed refreshed rather than exhausted by his day's progress. For eight days he maintained this strenuous fellowship with his new friends and in this time they had traversed a wide circle, bringing them back to their first meeting-place.

At the evening fire, Elijah tried again to tell of the growth of his conviction.

"It will appear nonsense to you, who have known me for so short a time: but I must harden my body if I am to respond to the 'Voice.'" He paused and there was a slight response from the oldest of the company. "All must answer their voices in their own ways. Rest here a day or two when we leave you. You will suffer no harm and I leave you with one brief counsel: sleep by day and awake to the speaking of the stars at night. They will whisper their wisdom."

The morning saw their departure and he was not to see them again for many years.

He awoke at night-fall. For the whole day after his friends' departure, he had slept the deep sleep of physical exhaustion, seemingly dreamless and undisturbed. He awoke refreshed and saw a little above the horizon the blaze of the evening star, a diamond-sun above the palms. He shifted on his cloak and lay on his back, his eyes gradually accustomed to the new intensity of starlight. He began to isolate the constellations, repeating to himself the childhood names and their legends. Even his mind became silent and wordless and as he looked directly above him he began to participate in the slow wheeling of the heavens. The clash of the stars within the constellation seemed now no longer silent but to bring him a sound he had never heard except in the Torah readings – the cymbal-clash of many bells. It was a harmony at the highest limit of human hearing, beyond the notes of the bat at night; beneath the harmony he heard another deeper sound, the movement of earth, steady from its first creation, and his mind, in the long hours, added the song of the 'Sons of the Morning' and he murmured in response, "and in the depths be praise."

"Father, if in the simplicity of our minds we were confined to one sole belief, what would it be?"

In the months that followed Elijah's return from the desert oases, Jokanan, their mentor in Torah saw beyond the burnt features, the hardened muscles of this new young man, to another, deeper toughening. His words were as spare as ever but when he spoke, in the simplicity, the apparent naivety of his words, there was an exploration which hinted at many hours of solitary thought. Questions sometimes appeared incomprehensible, even absurd but on this occasion Jokanan

22

responded to a real craving in the rapidly maturing voice.

"We are rarely granted the luxury of one solitary matter of belief but if we were so confined – stripped as it were for a race or a long and bitter struggle – then the answer lies in words that have been on your tongue every evening and morning since childhood: 'Thou shalt love the Lord thy God.' "

"Those words I have indeed spoken day after day – and I have never understood them, never truly spoken them with my heart and understanding. My memories of my mother, my care for my father, for my brother Reuven – all these I can love, see before me, part of my very self. And my friends, and above them all, you Jokanan, all of you I can love. But God! I reverence the name, have heard you speak of 'the mighty works' but as I look beyond the infinite distances of the desert, look up to those vast spaces between the stars, I know that He is there, to be worshipped – but loved? If I admitted 'love', I should seem to reduce him to our level, a being fitted for the life of Tishbe."

"Even that may also come in His infinite compassion. But we live in our human patience, singing the songs of that splendid singer of Israel. But Elijah, I have one thing to tell you, no comfort for you but perhaps a heavier burden than you have yet known. Your name, yes, quite simply your name. I have often marvelled at the boldness of your naming, the simple courage of your father as he marked you out by your name. Elijah: '*God is God*' – no more but simply that. 'God is God', as though by your name and nothing more, you were to carry through life the profoundest of man's knowledge. That may well be why you stumble over 'Love the Lord your God.' Yours is a more austere declaration and it may be all you have to say. 'God is God' from all ages and to all ages."

23

The climb was harsh and he had not attempted it since childhood. The flock had been left with Reuven on the lower slopes and with no explanation beyond a gesture towards the upper reaches, he began the long climb to the summit.

At his first resting-place, Tishbe was still in sight, a spare line of buildings spread along the delicate green of the lower valley. He then turned to the last steep ascent of the wadi and found himself on a plateau of boulders, split and crevassed by the sun's heat and the sharp cold of the upland nights. Then came the precipitous slopes to the three peaks which topped the range. He made for the middle peak and found that this was no longer scrambling but a true climb, where every yard of ascent was won by precarious foothold and the aching pull of his arms. He paused at a ledge which gave him a little respite and searched for the next series of toe- and hand-holds. Dusk was already upon him and the peak well above. In his weariness he made for a darker shadow on the cliff which suggested at least a shallow opening, perhaps a cleft in the rock. He won to it and found a downward-sloping break in the rock, an opening a little shorter than a man's length but offering at least a minimal shelter. Into this cleft he pressed his body, drew his arms and legs into some semblance of rest and composed himself for the dark.

He had not expected the numbing cold. At first it attacked his fingers, carelessly exposed at the edge of the rock, and he pressed his forearms between his thighs. Soon, through the light slumber he was aware of the ache through his whole body and knew for the first time the secret of the wilderness of tumbled rock: for through the silence of the night, no cry of predator or rustle of wind, there was, through the whole body of the rock, a minute sound of parting, the thrusting open of cracks through the whole body of seemingly invulnerable stone.

He had known the violence of heat at noon but had never realised its complement, the wedge-thrust of cold into the body of rock.

In the pale grey of dawn he was craving the sun's rays. When they came, out of the swiftly changing colours, eastward below him, there was no mitigation of the cold, but simply an urgency to renew the climb.

Within an hour he had reached the top. He could have told no-one the motive for the climb when he had set out from Tishbe. Now it was clear before him.

Below the narrow plateau which marked the summit stretched a wilderness of broken rock. Some miles to the west this gave way to sandy scrub which in turn led to a denser growth, dark green and formless at this distance. Through it there meandered a line of water again reduced by distance to a rivulet – the Jordan! And beyond, the wilderness and barren upland margin of Judah. There, in that distant and forbidding landscape, was his destiny. The many inarticulate promptings of these last months and years now formed themselves into one clear demand. There, in Judah and beyond was to be declared in all its stark simplicity, the clamour of the 'Voice' which declared his name, 'God is God.'

As he turned eastward, to begin his search for a less precipitous descent to the wadi, a shaft of sunlight picked out a peak, northward and to his left. It was a rounded mass rising sheer from the wilderness plain and the exclamation came unbidden: "Nebo!" It had always been for him, from childhood, a word of ill-omen. Moses – that giant of the beginning of history, to lead his people through the thunder of Sinai, the torment of desert, and then, as the generations had fallen away, to bring him to this torturing vision. To drive the lonely genius to the ascent of Nebo, to stand him there in his desolation and to show the failing eyes, across the waters of Jordan, the 'promised' land. Could God's irony be harsher? This was no promise, but an end, a death in dereliction.

Elijah turned away from the sight of Nebo and looked again westward to the misty outlines of Judah. Nebo informed his young eyes. He, with his one, scarcely coherent message for his people, could he expect more from the providence of Jahweh than the dereliction of Moses?

BOOK TWO

Omri had been a king mighty in battle and when, at his death, he was succeeded by Ahab, so like his father in appearance and ambitions, the omens seemed good for an eminent and prosperous reign. The land had been made fertile by careful husbandry, cities gathered wealth not only from their hinterland but from trade far beyond their bounds.

Indeed, stretching back into the years before Omri's reign, the genius of David still echoed in men's ears and the grandeur of Solomon lifted their hearts. When had the worship of Jahweh known such glory as in the Temple created by Solomon?

To the prophets of the Judean heights, those shepherds in the uplands whose gentle flocks gave them quiet leisure to think of the demands of God's will, one aspect of Solomon's building skills gave peculiar pleasure. It was his command that the process of creating the Temple and its precincts should be in complete silence. All stone was to be dressed at the quarry and carried silently on its final stage at the building-site. There were to be no unmannerly command as the materials were assembled; each builder, a skilled craftsman, knew his place and his actions without prompting. As teams of men lifted each mighty block of stone into place, the only sound was the stifled gasp of their breathing and the quiet

27

sibilance of their trowels as the slurry of thin cement was smoothed into place between each block.

And so it was as the interior was fashioned. The great balks of oak to gird ceilings and walls had been cut and dressed to fitting size at the place where they were felled. Lebanon, distant Lebanon provided cedar in plenty for the walls, both panels and carving, while each piece of timber was wedged and dowelled in silence, no hammer or mallet breaking the busy silence.

Here was their tradition of worship, the awe of sacrifice anticipated even while the place of sacrifice was in process of building. Jahweh was to be worshipped in a still solemnity and the prophets of the quiet hill pastures gloried in the promise that the voice of Jahweh would be heard in an attentive stillness. In their hearts they prayed that Ahab would be alert to all he had inherited, that with strong rule, and hopefully no great threat from the surrounding powers, flocks could be pastured in peace and the tillers of the lowlands be allowed their rest beneath their vine arbours.

But doubts soon grew. Ahab was content, it seemed, that the armies inherited from Omri should rest awhile in peace. His aim, it was said, was not the defeat of alien kings, nor treaties of defensive alliance with them, but the increase of his nation's wealth. Nothing more could reasonably be drawn from the field, and the flocks could explore no more pastures. There could be only one way to gather wealth greater than the king's treasury already had: foreign trade.

But where? Lands to the east of Jordan offered little prospect. Their agriculture was on thin soil, their flocks on scattered pasture and many were hardened nomads of the desert. There remained Phoenicia, rich in its own resources and fortunate in ports which gathered in all the wealth of the Great Sea. To Phoenicia Ahab turned his eyes.

28

The safest guarantee of assured and lasting trade was a marriage contract and an eminently desirable marriage was an immediate prospect, to a princess both beautiful and of great intellectual power. Jezebel of Tyre was the daughter of Ethbaal, King of Tyre and himself a priest of Asherah. The bond between Israel and Tyre in Phoenicia seemed thus assured and the alliance, profit sealed by piety, won substantial approval and an even richer future was foretold for the royal house.

Jezebel to our beloved cousin Jezratha in Sidon.

"The day came all too quickly. I was under no illusion about the marriage contract: I was an object of trade, a seal on a treaty with an alien and unloved people. What had we to do with these descendants of desert wanderers? Much more, what had we to do with the austere maleness of their god, Jahweh? What can they know of the ecstacy of our prayers and sacrifices, the burning of our words, as Baal-Melqart and Asherah are united more closely than lovers as we pray to them? I knew I was to be stifled even in the summit beauty of which they spoke, as they prepared my residence in Jezreel. This was to be exile – not from my father and my kin; priest and priestess, I should always be one with him, united to them – but exile from the groves, the high places, the trance and the ecstacy.

Then came the contract before the marriage day. My father had decreed for me the dress of a virgin-slave, a sheath of white from throat to instep, a simple girdle of gold-thread at my waist and my hair undressed and loose. There was to be but one woman of my attendants and she dressed in the plain garment of an Asherah-acolyte. He had but one attendant; both were dressed in the robes of Baal-Melqart prophets. We stood together in the ceremonial hall, a small group before the table on which the clay stood ready, the moulds and the stylus to our hands.

I believe – my servant told me later – that I schooled my

29

features to impassivity; if Asherah could not give me strength, to whose aid could she come?

One brief trumpet call and the doors were opened. The contrast took away all my practised gravity and I must have looked like a stricken infant! Two ceremonial bowmen entered, followed by a group – two by two they walked – of richly dressed youths, princelings I supposed. And then, my betrothed! I had thought little and expected less; why should a chattel debate its fate?

But here was a man! I believe even Asherah would have trembled, the grove been stirred at the sight of him. In a robe as severe as mine but cloth of gold, his belt a cincture of leather stained to the kingly purple; his hair, dark, long and almost without a ripple in its surface, was drawn back from his forehead and hung – unconfined even by a circlet, – to touch his shoulders. His features were sharp, his nose arched and his eyes, deep-set as those of a hunter, or a warrior used to command. I looked directly into his eyes – no bashful drooping of eyelids before this man – and as I looked he smiled, more inwardly than in greeting, as if he too had anticipated a conflict between us.

There was the exchange of ceremonial greeting and a few courtesies. The royal scribe came to the table and stamped out two tablets in the prepared clay. My father used the stylus firmly and with ceremony, flourishing the royal title at the head of each tablet; Ahab appended his device below my father's and the stylus was placed in my hand. I no longer looked at Ahab but bit my signature deep into the clay below his name.

There were no more words as each group turned to their several chambers.

How different the morrow's ceremonies. Much music, much laughter which penetrated even to my private chambers and heard through the chatter of preparations. Today there was to be no austerity, of a handmaid of Asherah. Today I was to be in the full stature and dignity of a Tyrian princess, crowned in readiness for a role, the complexity of which I was already understanding.

Conditions had been laid down by my father and readily assented to by Ahab – was he always to be thus malleable? –

30

and the first was immediately fulfilled. The sealing of the contract, with music, prayers and the incense-clouds, was to be in the full blaze of sun, with a simple awning at the entrance of the stone circle of Baal. There, in its slight shade, Ahab and I, my father – Baal's surrogate – and a priestess of Asherah, were to make and consecrate our vows.

Our two several processions gathered to the sacred place and again, in the silence as the courtiers converged, I looked for the second time into the eyes of Ahab – and I found what I had looked for. There was admiration and desire there; he explored my features as though my face were an alien territory; and then his eyes wandered to the Baal-grove, the standing-stones and the shrub-knots overshadowed by the sacred oaks. His eyes wavered, as though a dismaying thought had invaded the ceremony. Then his eyes returned to mine; there was consideration there and in the furrows of his forehead, calculation as of a commander on a plain who sees his adversary on a height before him. Then he smiled and I knew the conflict was over.

The ceremony completed, the second condition remained to be fulfilled. Before we returned to the royal chambers, I had stipulated that Ahab and I should go, unattended, to the grove of Asherah – for was not I her priestess and about to explore alien groves? It was no great distance and a few minutes saw us at the entrance before the laurels closed us in. There our union was the coupling of royal beasts and I wondered as we returned: would the priests and the prophets of Jahweh give their assent?"

Ahab the King to his chamberlain and chief scribe at the summer palace in Jezreel.

"We stay for the remainder of this spring of the year in our city of Samaria. Make all ready for our coming to Jezreel. The instruments of music will already be with you and their players well lodged. Have ready at our command artificers, gardeners and slaves to labour, awaiting the demands of our Queen, Jezebel

31

*of Tyre, for all she may require of their skills. The five weeks to
our arrival will suffice for these preparations."*

There was high speculation in Jezreel. The beauty of
Jezebel had been spoken of over the weeks since the
ceremonies at Tyre and there were other hints. Ahab
was as kingly as his father Omri on a field of battle; at
the shaping of a trade treaty or political alliance he was
beyond compare, and at the offerings, the prayers, the
psalms to God? Here the head-shakings, the mutterings
and forebodings grew ominous. Was the crown of Ahab
as regal as the coronet of Jezebel?

At each nightfall it became the custom for small
parties of young men to go to the eastern wall of the
city, there to speculate on the day and night activity in
the fields beyond. An army of labourers was digging
and trenching over many acres in a wide circle; at its
centre stood many hundreds of laurel bushes, each root-
ball covered in rough cloth, and among them, young
but mature oaks, also ready for the planting. A forest-
grove seemed in the planning and there were troubled
whispers among the young men.

Then came further rumours. Beyond the broken fields
and the preparations for planting, another army of
workmen was labouring in a great crescent which
embraced the projected grove. They worked to a clear
pattern, a geometry of rectangles, trenched deep into
the soil. At intervals pits had been dug into the underlying clay and great quantities were puddled in huge vats
at the outer perimeter. The purpose was clear to the
young men, as they saw row upon row of bricks laid
out to dry in the sun. But for what purpose was this
great suburb being built, what invasion was anticipated?
– for Jezreel was jealous of its size and beauty and

32

no great spread of building had been foretold in its planning.

Four of the young men, more troubled even than their fellows, waited until the ceremonies of Sabbath were over and went at dawn to the small vineyard of Joseph, a young vine-dresser who had determined to begin a walled garden of his own. From his orphaned boyhood he had laboured for Naboth, a generous land-owner, who cultivated an extensive vineyard on the southern slopes beyond the Jezreel wall and below the sunny walks of the royal palace. There Joseph had learned his trade under expert eyes: to strike cuttings of ripe wood and to graft and bud the finer varieties; to prepare the coarse soil in which the vines flourished and to follow the arduous and delicate art of pruning; all this Naboth had lovingly watched, for he recognised in Joseph an innate skill which might one day take over his own inheritance, for he was childless.

Joseph had an equal concern for Naboth. The pos-session of such extensive vineyards had been a continu-ous charge on a frame of precarious health. Though he was still in the prime of years, the vineyards had needed increasing care, and it had fallen to Joseph to see to the strengthening of the wind-break at the northern boundary of his land. Naboth was the fifth generation of the vineyard's owners; the founder of the plantation, a century and a half before Naboth's day, had prudently planted olive-trees at the north-eastern extremity of the land and these, in their gnarled maturity, were now a profitable wind-break. The gathering of the olives each year did not compare with the grape harvest but the olive-press was busy and supplied enough oil for the family and servants, with some left over for trade.

But the olive-trees needed shelter themselves, if the winds from the northern hills were to be effectively broken. Joseph had seen this in his apprentice-years and had taken an early initiative in planting poplar and ash beyond the line of olives. Pollarded, these supplied poles for the lines of vine-branches, and in their maturity established a mild shelter which benefited both olive and grape. In all this, Naboth deemed himself fortunate in his fostering of Joseph, now more a son than an apprentice-labourer.

But there had been an increasing change in Joseph. Year by year his eye had been keener for the quality of the grapes, quick to detect the vines on which the grapes could be allowed longer to mature, even to raisin quality, ready to tell the workers the precise day on which the harvest should begin and, above all, wary for the least sign of mildew or pest which should imperil future harvests. In all this, Naboth could detect nothing but a growth in responsible maturity and he began to look forward to the day when he could withdraw to the tranquillity of his home at the city wall and allow sun and shadow to show him the seasonal changes in his fruitful acres.

At the same time he became aware of a change beyond maturity in the character of Joseph; his work each day, each season, seemed to be accomplished with a casual ease, an effortlessness which could be the reward of his growing maturity but which equally might indicate another preoccupation. There was also – and Naboth didn't grudge this in any way – an increase in Joseph's requests for days which would free him from work in the vineyard.

One autumn, as the harvest and the pressing of the grapes was complete, Joseph asked Naboth at evening, as they sat together in the arbour at the side of the house, whether he might now beg a week's absence from the vineyard to pursue his own affairs. Naboth felt secure enough in Joseph's trust in him to question this more substantial request.

34

"You are beginning to feel the need for your own settled home, perhaps your own vineyard to establish – for a family, a wife?"

Joseph smiled his appreciation of the question. "Yes, perhaps a vineyard, if you will allow me to take from our nursery of young vines. I think now I could establish such a planting as your near neighbour and still have time and strength to oversee your workers. But no wife as yet! There is a more pressing concern."

Naboth realised a new gravity in the young man's look and voice, and waited for him to gather his thoughts.

"It's not an easy thing to talk about. I believe I have no words to tell you of this part of my life. You know that in these last years I have asked you more and more often to release me for days from my duties; I have tried to arrange these on the eve of Sabbath and before dawn I have set out as swiftly as I could to make for the desolate hill country between Jezreel and Samaria. There I have made new friends – not many but warm and loyal – shepherds with their small flocks, wandering from well to spring, from one pasturage to another. They are hardy people, proud of wresting a living from the unkind uplands and wholly loyal to each other. I have longed each time I leave them, for the next Sabbath when I can join them again."

Naboth realised that the break in Joseph's explanation indicated no end to his thought; there was clearly much more to be said and he allowed Joseph to find the words.

"The flocks would be gathered at Sabbath-eve in sheltered valleys where rough folds had been built by each shepherd for his flock. A fire marked their central meeting-place and there I learnt a new meaning in worship, a new insight into Torah. We remained silent together for perhaps an hour or longer. Then one would speak quietly in the words of David of the sun, moon and stars 'which He had ordained' and in company with

35

the others I would search the firmament. On still nights there was no movement of cloud through which the moon would sail but out of the heavens would come an almost silent harmony, the voices of the stars in their courses.

"Or another would speak of pasture by still waters and in the silence would pursue his thought and then tell us – 'No king is a king who is not a shepherd' and I would begin to question Samaria, Jezreel, as the halting-places 'by still waters.' And so the day would dawn and we knew the peace of Sabbath."

Naboth's intuition and his affection for the young man told him that Joseph had still not reached the heart of the matter, that silent patience was still needed.

"I counted myself too young to speak in that noble company but there came a night when words – not mine – seemed to spring to my throat. One of the older shepherds smiled and raised his hand for silence. The words clamoured in my throat but without utterance until my eyes were caught by those of the old man. Then I spoke:

'Hear, O Israel; the Lord thy God is one God; and thou shalt love.'

"The words halted on my tongue. These words which I had spoken with all Israel, every morning and evening, aloud or in the silence of prayer, were now new words; I had never spoken them before. 'One God, one sole God, alone from and to eternity' – this was the harmony, the angelic song which rang out below the so customary words, 'Hear, O Israel.' I was silent and looked about me at the shepherds gathered there. All of them looked at me, their youngest, and there was smiling in their eyes; and then the eldest spoke:

"Joseph our son, these are the words of prophecy that you speak, the very heart of prophecy. All Israel repeats these words every day but for few, even in Israel, do the words have meaning. That is the fate of prayer, to become mere patter. We" – he looked around at the shepherds gathered about me – "We are shepherds by trade and prophets by vocation and you are numbered among us. I see by your hands that you are no shepherd. The stains there are the blood of the grape and this too is a noble trade. Shepherd and vinedresser – there can be no greater foundation for prophecy; Messiah himself, when he comes, may be content tenderly to lead his sheep, or tread the wine-press.

"You, beyond your knowledge, have learned your lesson, your entry into prophecy; from this day onwards you will have only one word to declare: 'Your God is *one* God, your God *alone.*' "

"Naboth, I come to you with that message. No!" – he halted Naboth's words – "No! I wish never to leave your neighbourhood. Yes, I will establish my humble vineyard as near to yours as you will permit. And there I shall work and learn more of my craft; but there will be demands. These shepherd-prophets will not need to order my ways. The voice will demand its speech – 'One God – one God alone' – and that will suffice."

Naboth said nothing but smiled and placed his hand on Joseph's shoulder. Together they left the valley prospect and went to their rest.

Tishbe remained a quiet village, well removed from the main highways, content to be 'beyond Jordan' and in peace. Elijah still tended his few sheep but seemed to his family to haunt more and more the solitudes of the high crags. He spoke little but when the silences became even longer, he would leave Tishbe for days at a time and make for the desert oases, returning with renewed tranquillity in his eyes.

Then one day he set out not eastwards but to the

north. He strode rapidly to the lower bank of the Kerith and looked across to the unwelcoming northern limits of the valley. He went down to the water-course – the stream was scarcely two yards across – and followed its bank until he had walked westward for about an hour. He knew that still further west was the Jordan valley, which he had never approached, with no wish to cross to strange territory; he knew too that if the Brook Kerith were to join Jordan, there must be a cleft in that massive and sombre range before him. This was the object of his search.

He had brought rough fare for a week's wanderings and he followed the stream – noting with a shepherd's eye the occasional wide stretches of pasture where Kerith flooded – but pressing on to the wilder rocks beyond. The stream had cut deep and the sandstone had in places been penetrated to the underlying limestone shelves. These tougher rocks made flatter gorges in the stream's sculpturing and as he pursued its course, Elijah saw that tributary streams had also cut through the sandstone layers and had even gouged out caves in the limestone beds. Thoughts of Adullam and the rocky shelters of the fleeing David came involuntarily to his mind and obscurely he realised the purpose of these days. Without any conscious reason for fear, he knew with certainty that one day flight might be a necessity for him, that an En-gedi might have to be found for him in the security of Kerith.

It was the more disquieting that he could not formulate a fear. There was no cause of which he was aware, that would create danger for him or the people of Tishbe. His 'Voice' was a companion to daily routine, an assurance that beyond the ordinary, the securing of shelter and pasture, there was another mode of being. But the 'Voice' went no further, issued no warning.

He pushed on through the intersecting breaks in the

crags until he reached their highest point. The landscape before him had a rain-washed clarity and for the first time he saw way beyond the Jordan Valley to the further interior. Features could not be distinguished, though colour-tone seemed of infinite variety, and the spreading green below the further uplands and beyond the wilderness seemed to Elijah to promise a land richer than any this side of Jordan. He knew from hearsay that flanking the vista to north and south were the two 'capital cities' of Samaria and Jezreel. There the house of Omri still ruled, for Ahab now inherited. All seemed well but the ways beyond Jordan were of little concern to him and to his kin. In this assurance but with obscure questionings below the surface of thought, he made his way back to Tishbe.

The young men continued to monitor the activity beyond the walls of Jezreel and there came a day in early summer when the circular area was wholly planted and the crescent of dwellings roofed. So dense was the planting of laurels that the oaks seemed to spring from a sea of green. Three paths appeared to radiate eastward from the centre of the grove, with another single path directed to the wall of Jezreel and its eastern gate. Where the four paths met, the young men could see the sheen of water, seemingly a large cistern or bathing-place and on the grass at its bank a single massive pillar of stone stood erect.

Their watch was now continuous day and night and after some days, they saw in the evening light a great deal of activity among the small buildings beyond the grove, the hurrying to and fro of robed figures and there were brief and indistinct bursts of pipe-music and the almost inaudible rhythm of drums. They felt a new urgency in their watching and one of them ran to fetch

Joseph from his dwelling at Naboth's vineyard. Together they looked out over the changed scene and Joseph's lips curled as if at a bitter and distasteful drink.

"Wait here and keep your watch." After the urgent command, Joseph returned and, waking Naboth, told him of his fears, that an alien obscenity was prepared for Jezreel to endure. He said that he wished to consult his friends in the hills and with Naboth's assent, strode off to see how many he could find.

Two had made their night-encampment at no great distance from the hill of Jezreel itself. Joseph explained his fears and the rumours which filled the city. Obscurely, he and his friends sensed that Jezebel was preparing an affront to Israel, a break in their very history. Joseph told them that he was wholly at their command to do what seemed best to them.

"A clear mind has always demanded the desert ways. It is now some years since word came from beyond Jordan that the spirit of God had breathed on a young shepherd, a son of Tishbe. Kin of mine, friends of the wandering desert folk, had word of him, that he spoke of a 'Voice' but that the words were few and of a seeming simplicity. We counsel you, Joseph, that you go beyond Jordan and tell Elijah – so I believe he is called – of your fears and all you have seen beyond Jezreel. It may be that 'the Voice' will speak with greater clarity to you."

It was a strange and disquieting journey. The steady half-run east from Jezreel to the Jordan valley left Joseph wholly without any clear idea of his mission to Elijah; indeed, it seemed to him that his shepherd-friends were relying altogether too firmly on rumour about this Tishbite, seen by none of them. He was then preoccupied with finding a ford across Jordan and then a way, rarely traversed, through the dense and treacherous growth, half shrub, half noxious herbs, on the east side of the river. The greatest hardship in the steamy heat was the attack from the clouds of flies disturbed by his progress.

He came out at a defile between the escarpment of Kerith and the village of Tishbe and a shepherd directed him to the quickest path to Elijah's home. His mind was now settled that he could do no more than identify himself as a vine-dresser of Jezreel, a friend of shepherds in the uplands who had prophetic powers, and a simple narrative of all that he and the young men of Jezreel had observed in recent weeks in the city environs. He was also clear in his mind that beyond the bare fact that Ahab was married to Jezebel, a Tyrian princess, no word should be spoken by him which should prejudice Elijah's judgment.

He arrived at early evening and inquiry for Elijah took him to his home, where the shepherd was seated at the entrance to the house. At Joseph's appearance, Elijah stood to greet him and Joseph's surprise was scarcely concealed. Elijah was sparely, even meanly dressed, a softly-cured skin covering his left shoulder and falling to his calves, a rough mantle, seemingly woven of camel-hair, thrown over his right shoulder. He appeared burnt to extreme leanness by hard work in open sun but, with no spare flesh, his torso, thighs and calves rippled with a warrior's muscle, ready for immediate and violent action if it were called for. All this was a swift appraisal but immediately the smiling face required a deeper assessment. This was not the countenance of a day-labourer; toil there must have been, to furnish those limbs but the quiet eyes spoke of long patience, a tranquil waiting until events should show their demand. His eyes penetrated Joseph's gaze; his high cheekbones, firm and yet mobile mouth, arched nose and jutting chin were

41

framed in a dark chestnut mane (the word, Joseph thought, was inevitable) which fell below his shoulders and had the clear sheen of hair carefully tended. He held himself with the poised expectancy of a young David waiting for Goliath's first move.

Joseph realised that before this secure stance he had nothing to say and it fell to Elijah to break in silence with a host's courtesy.

"You are welcome, stranger. Before speech between us, it would seem you need cleansing and refreshment. You have crossed rough places and gathered mud on your way!"

Joseph was astonished again by the rich modulation of this voice. It would surely be an instrument to carry far, in mountain or across a plain. A gesture indicated a seat at the door and leaving him only briefly, Elijah returned with water and a towel. Kneeling at his guest's feet and, first brushing away the caked mud, the burrs and thorns which clung to his feet and ankles, he washed them gently, poured clean water over his guest's hands and placed cloths at his side. Without a word he entered the house again and returned with a platter of barley cakes and two goblets of wine. In silence they took the meal, as much ceremony as refreshment.

"You have travelled far."

"From Jezreel." At the name of the city, Elijah's smile ceased and with hard eyes and a sudden sharpness which took all harmony from the voice, he said:

"Your eyes tell of ill news, even tragedy. What have you to say to us, to us who live aside from the stirrings of your world?"

"I should first in courtesy tell you of myself. Since boyhood I have served Naboth a vine-dresser, the noblest and most admired man of Jezreel, and I believe I may say that I have become like a son to him. I have also other friends in the remoter uplands, poorer but no less

42

noble than Naboth, tending humble flocks of sheep, but wise in the Law and the heavens and truly filled with the power of prophets. And they tell me – and Naboth does not deny it, – that I have the voice of prophecy, though I have little to say beyond this, that God is one God and must be loved."

Elijah was silent and scrutinised Joseph's features.

"There seems little here which speaks of tragic haste and a toilsome journey. You seem in all ways a fortunate young man!"

Joseph gave no response to the half-question nor to the smile that went with it.

"In past years Naboth would have told you that he who lived in Jezreel was indeed a fortunate man. The fairest possible site in a fair country and honoured to be the summer residence of kings. Now we question this. Ahab has brought to us a Tyrian princess, Jezebel his bride, a woman of great beauty and – so they tell me who move on the fringes of the court – of powerful mind and speech. Ahab is a warrior and a diplomat but is no match for this remarkable woman. She rules in Samaria and Jezreel!"

"And worships?"

"Her father, King of Tyre, is a priest of Baal and she, it seems, a priestess of Asherah."

"And has left her country, her kin and her worship and now falls before God, as a bride should?"

"Indeed, no! Our young men, faithful to God and jealous of his worship, have kept watch on the walls of the city and seen, in its immediate neighbourhood, a grove planted, with a standing-stone, as of an altar to Baal. Outside the grove are many new dwellings from which paths traverse the grove to its centre. And as I left, it was on all men's lips –"

Elijah rose to his feet, his face transfigured in anger and seemed ready to strike even the messenger himself.

43

"And it was on all men's lips?"

"That to those dwellings beyond the grove had come four hundred and fifty prophets of Baal-Melqart, four hundred priests of Asherah and attendant women for the ritual fornications in the grove."

Elijah again rose to his feet. Anger had gone from his eyes, his face a blank mask. He rose from his stool, went into the house and brought blankets to the sheltered entrance and spread them as a bed.

"Sleep as soundly as your journey has merited. Before dawn you journey again."

Elijah knew a more comfortable route and crossing of Jordan and the two men were soon in the wilderness beyond the valley. Their first day and half the night saw them at the entrance to the long valley of Jezreel and they slept out the rest of the night. At dawn, *Shema* and the morning psalms brought peace for breaking their fast and brief talk before the ascent to the city, which they hoped to reach at sundown or at least at early star-light.

"You told me, diffidently as becomes a young man, that you too were deemed a prophet. God grants you a vision? You hear the echo of his voice?"

"No vision and indeed few words from the voice; but since I have heard him, in the stillness with my shepherd-friends beneath the stars, the words we have just spoken together have taken a new meaning, an urgency, 'Hear, O Israel, your God is One, *alone.*'"

"I also am deemed a prophet and yet I don't venture even to the *Shema.* I have only my name to declare, my own herald, to trumpet nothing but my name: 'God is Jahwch', 'Jahweh is God'; 'God is God alone!'"

"That is surely a sufficient trumpet-call and walls may yet topple at the sound."

The day was arduous as they made for Jezreel, the sun unrelenting and the way hard. They arrived, as Joseph had anticipated, in early starlight and he took Elijah to his home beside Naboth's vineyard and they slept the remainder of the night through.

In the early morning they went to take counsel of Naboth, who had little of comfort to tell them. Preparations at and beyond the grove had gone on swiftly, there was much music of pipes and harps at nightfall and harsh singing from the heart of the grove. There were rumours, perhaps, Naboth thought inspired by Ahab's courtiers, to soften men's minds, that a notable announcement was to be made within days.

Meanwhile, it was Naboth's counsel, that Joseph should return quietly to his daily work and Elijah to seek out the upland prophets who were eagerly waiting for him.

His coming – and indeed the absence of Joseph for the best part of a week – could not be kept secret and it was assumed by all that this strange man from across Jordan would at once join the prophets in the country. There was excited anticipation of their meeting and its outcome. Would royal notice be taken of it? And was not this Elijah a strange and enigmatic creature? Of a beauty and stature to recall David in his prime and yet so forbidding in much of his appearance; his hair unbound and free, and yet of such beauty that a girl might envy him; his body taut and controlled as a warrior's and yet dressed in nothing but a skin for his shoulder and loins and a mantle rough-woven of camel hair. In his presence you were aware only of his eyes, whether they smiled or blazed in anger; in his absence you remembered nothing but a frightening crudity of power, the coiled strength of a lion before it leapt.

He spent a day in the upland pastures, listening to the prophets and their forebodings. In a strange way, as they and their fellows crossed and re-crossed these sheep-tracks, they became better informed, with more variety of viewpoint, than their friends in Jezreel who were nearer the events. As they spoke to Elijah, all realised that the worship of Israel was in greater danger than at any time since the women of Philistia threatened its sanctity.

They were interrupted by an unexpected visitor, who approached them with a courtly grace they found repellent, and who spoke with arrogant assurance.

"They tell me that in this honourable company I might find Elijah the Tishbite." He gave the title an insulting twist.

"They told you truth." Elijah, standing in his full height, towered over the courtling.

"Your message to the Tishbite?"

"The noble Queen Jezebel of Tyre and Israel, Mistress of Jezreel and priestess of Asherah, commands your presence at the entrance from Jezreel to the sacred grove of Asherah. She commands converse with the Tishbite at dawn tomorrow."

"No-one 'commands' the Tishbite, whether tomorrow or at any other time. But I will render her a courtesy which she shows so scantilly. I shall be at the gate of Jezreel at dawn."

The first rays of the sun cast the shadows of the tall oaks on the three steps down to the grove, as Elijah stood on the mosaic floor of the portico. He was without motion or expression on his features as he waited. From the centre of the grove came Jezebel, dressed as simply as in the ceremony before her marriage; without ostentation, she was queen and priestess and of calm beauty in the early light. She waited for his acknowledgment of her regality.

46

"You are silent, Tishbite and scant of the honour due to your queen. You will descend from your eminence and walk with me in the grove as we speak of Israel."

"I have to enter the houses of my friends this day and their hearths would be polluted if the sole of my foot had touched that ground."

"You speak arrogantly and harshly, Tishbite; the tone is not seemly."

"I have no doubt that you will hear harsher tones from me, if our acquaintance lasts."

There was silence between them; swords had made their first contact but the bout was not yet begun. The queen looked at the man before her, calculating his manhood and the degree of his resistance.

"You are comely, Elijah, wasted on the desert sand and rock!"

"And you, Jezebel, you understand the truths of the desert?"

"Jezebel!" The word blazed her affront. "I am your queen and a priestess of your people's religion!"

"No queen of mine and I recognise no 'priestess.' "

Jezebel had enough knowledge of courtly conflict to realize that her adversary was formidable. On alien ground and with no more than a contract asserting her claim, she realised here the desert-bred qualities that Tyre had never matched. With inherited skill, she withdrew from open conflict.

"There has been little time for me to learn the faith and the ways of Jahweh – and Ahab is a preoccupied and unskilled tutor! Cease your frowning, Elijah and Jezebel may attend on your wisdom."

The sentence had begun in irony but before Elijah's gaze there was a faltering in her voice. Were there no breaches in this citadel? For the first time in her mature experience she realised the impotence of her beauty, that her mind alone in its suppleness could pursue this

47

duel. In face of Elijah's silence, her voice dropped almost to pleading.

"I have much to learn, Elijah and, if Baal and Asherah will, much to teach. Tell me of the ways of Jahweh."

"He flies on the wings of the wind, is enthroned on the clouds of heaven, measures the firmament with the single span of his hand and his voice – do you wish to hear of his voice?"

She recognised the irony in every phrase, knew that she was treated as a child and with a child's angry petulance, she demanded:

"Tell me of the voice."

Elijah's tone changed. There was almost regret in his words as he looked down at the arrogant but so fragile beauty of the woman before him. For a moment she ceased to be an opponent and seemed a child needing instruction; how much could she compass?

"There have been thunder-claps that have more stillness than the sound of God's voice; lightning flashes are paled by one glance from his eyes; and yet one breeze from the desert wastes, a breath that scarcely ruffles the sand-ripples, carries more sound than the whisper of his voice – and I long to hear that whispered word."

"And if you heard that word, what would it say?"

"No more than my name: 'Elijah' – 'Jahweh is God; God is Jahweh' – no more than that, for that is all I need to hear."

She met the declaration with incomprehension, for nothing in her upbringing had prepared her for this profound simplicity. As Elijah stood without breaking the complete immobility he had held, since he waited for her in the dawning, Jezebel dropped her eyes to the ground and there was a long silence.

"You will now learn of me, Elijah, learn of my devotion, the might of Baal-Melqart and the glorious beauty of Asherah. You would declare us to be of

48

mankind, you and I, but I am Jezebel and you Elijah, two distincts, two demands – and two mysteries! Never can man and woman divine their mysteries and in this darkness of 'no-knowledge', my father in his manhood is a priest of Asherah and I in my womanhood revere and serve Baal-Melqart. In the exchange of our mysteries we are of mankind, one in the darkness and one in the ecstacy. Do you understand this, Elijah the Tishbite, prophet of your single male Godhead?"

Elijah remained in his stillness and she was taken back to childhood, her nurse taking her to a secluded bay near Tyre. She knew the tideless movements of the Great Sea but on this day wind had been sufficiently powerful to send waves to the shore where she stood. To her right was a rock, a favourite bench on which she sat to listen to her nurse's stories but she was fearful this morning; the waves would surely destroy her rock. But it stood firm and the waters withdrew.

"You have nothing to say to Baal and Asherah?"

"There is no-one there to whom I can speak. You tell me of Tyrian deities; another might tell me of the Gods of Joppa, of Ashdod or Ashkelon, or cry aloud the secrets of those deities that dwell between the Rivers. You speak of landlords! Your worship is a sham. I have no more to say than this: God created heaven and earth and he rules, *alone* over all his creation. Jahweh is God, God is God alone!"

There was nobility in her defeat. Her wincing at his attack was little more than a passing frown and as he looked at her, with the slightest trace of a reluctant admiration, he saw her gather herself, saw the smile which touched only her lips and left the eyes implacable.

"You teach glibly, Tishbite! If I judge your speech aright, yours is a God of war and you his field-commander! But have a care to your forces. I have no more than this to say to you. Ahab this day issues a

49

proclamation, rumours of which, I'm told, have reached your uncouth friends in the hills. Baal-Melqart and Asherah are the *sole* gods of this land, their altars to crown all the high places. The altars of Jahweh are to be destroyed, and recalcitrant prophets and priests slaughtered. This is the will of Ahab, of Jezebel and their Gods."

Elijah moved forward one pace, flung his mantle over his left shoulder and with his right arm extended, began to speak in a low voice:

"This grove will wither, your body will be shattered, your 'gods' will perish and over all there shall reign, in power and in peace, the Lord God of Abraham, Isaac and Israel and his kingdom shall never end to all eternity."

His voice had risen to a trumpet-call and in the dimness of the grove there sounded a sighing and a rustling as the unseen listeners bowed, not in worship but in fear. In a tone of direct conversation, Elijah turned to Jezebel:

"You and your minions have heard my words. Jezreel needs to hear no more. The word of God has now to be declared in the city of Samaria and in that word may there be peace in all this troubled land."

Rumours of this conflict of words spread like a fire among thorns throughout the environs of Jezreel and Elijah spent two days with the shepherd-prophets of the hills as he prepared for Samaria. It was already clear to them, as small numbers of warriors spread in every direction from the fortress of Jezreel, that all God's prophets should disperse and take what shelter they could find in the heights and the hill-caves about them. The friends of Joseph now looked to Elijah as their hope in these tragic times, for in these few days to the west

50

of Jordan, Elijah had grown to a formidable stature and an intensity they had not before expected. To Joseph's bemused eyes and ears, Elijah's very garments had taken on a wilderness roughness, his voice a penetrating harshness which carried menace. But in the quiet evening as they prepared for their prayers before sleep, the prophets saw a deep compassion in Elijah's eyes as he gathered them about him.

"Tomorrow I leave for Samaria; where but in the city of Omri can God's declaration for his people be proclaimed?"

"And the words of proclamation? Dare you speak openly, with Ahab's soldiers abroad?"

"I am in no danger until the words are heard; after that, we are entirely in His hands."

The east was still grey with unlit cloud as Elijah set out for Samaria. It was wholly unfamiliar country to him and he followed where he could, the sheep-tracks of the highest ridges. A young shepherd had set him on his way but he was soon left behind as Elijah steadily increased his pace. He rested briefly and took little food and reached the outskirts of Samaria before sure word of Ahab's intention had reached its people.

As Elijah entered the gates of Samaria he cried aloud to those standing by:

"Gather all the people on the slopes to the north of the city. I have word from God which must be heard by all men."

Rumour and fear spread throughout the streets and markets, for the coming of Jezebel as queen of Israel had already been spoken of with disquiet. And word had reached them in recent weeks that there were disturbing happenings in Jezreel, even that the prophets and priests were in danger of death. Strange Baals were rumoured and if rumour was true, what should happen to the land of Israel? When they reached the plateau,

51

they saw Elijah standing and waiting for the crowd to gather and be still. His cry, when it came, had an appalling impersonality; in the days that followed they said fearfully among themselves that he seemed less a man than a strange instrument of a power they could not divine. The words came with rough force and still there were tones which declared peace beyond the menace, as though a conqueror cried 'Shalom' over his drawn sword:

"Hear, O Israel.
The Lord God of Abraham, Isaac and Israel
speaks in my words.
Hear, O Israel!
There shall not be dew nor rain these years
but according to my word.
The clouds will flee;
The dews will fail;
Springs will dry
And rivers cease their flowing.
Cattle will low at their troughs,
Sheep seek the pools in vain.
And over all there shall be drought and famine.
Hear, O Israel:
Pray, and pray again,
And pray that your prayers be heard,
That some may live,
That the nation shall sustain its heritage
And God be heard above the wailing.
This is the word of God."

There was no stirring in the multitude; many fell on their faces and slowly the words of prayer rose from among them. Women, as they clutched their children, looked fearfully at a sky which already looked like burnished brass, no cloud within their sight.

Elijah looked at the multitude, raised his arms in farewell and begun swiftly his way eastward.

BOOK THREE

The return to Tishbe was broken. Elijah had arranged with Joseph that he should meet a group of the prophets in the hills south of Jezreel. His journey there was sombre. It was not simply that he found himself drained of energy after the Samaria prophecy; that, for some hours had left him unmanned, with no more strength than would allow him to leave the environs of Samaria and seek a degree of safety in the wilderness of hills. He knew an urge within him to see for the first time the sacred 'high places', the altars where God had been honoured for so many generations. In the simplicities of Tishbe and the austerity of desert visions he had formed only a dim understanding of the worship of God in the land where cities vied with the rough places to give a sharper significance to the worship.

He had crossed two transverse ridges north of Samaria and thought it safe to seek the first sanctuary made holy by sacrifice in past ages. He had been told that in a clearing within a substantial stand of pines, a little off the road towards Dothan he would find one of the holiest of these shrines. He was content to be deflected north of his route towards the Jordan, for it would at length bring him within a few hours' journey of his meeting with Joseph and news of Jezreel.

He found the pines and rested a while in their shade

and in the comfort of the softer ground. Soon he thought he heard a distant chanting. Pushing further into the pine-wood, he found the clearing with its group of rough stones placed as an altar in the centre. The sounds of chanting – no more, he reckoned than five or six voices – were now nearer and at length a small group of rough-clad figures came to the stone altar and laid on the topmost stone a small dish in which a bed of charcoal smoked. When they were assembled about the altar, each in turn threw upon the burning charcoal a sprinkling of incense. The clouds of fragrance that came towards Elijah seemed to mingle happily with the resinous smell of the pines and he was about to come out to join them in the chanting of a psalm which had now begun, when he was halted by a clash of swords from the opposite side of the clearing. Before he could move, some twenty lightly-armed footsoldiers rushed into the clearing and within minutes all five of the prophets lay dead before the altar. This latest sacrifice of blood told Elijah more than he wished to know of the affairs of Jezreel and the determination of Jezebel to reply to his challenge. The struggle was clearly engaged but could not yet be in open field.

When the sound of armour had died away, Elijah went to the bodies in the clearing, disposed them reverently together before the altar, scattered the burning incense over them, prayed at their feet and continued his journey, his sorrow at the tragedy overborne by a determined anger. This blood should consecrate the forces of God.

Elijah was now some five hours' journeying from his meeting-point with Joseph and he wondered what tragedy might have overtaken his friends. He slackened his pace from his headlong progress from Samaria and gave himself time to consider his words with Joseph and the others. He determined also to risk a swift, night-time visit to Jezreel itself, for Naboth should be seen and his stay at the city debated between them.

He descended towards the valley of Jezreel and then climbed once more into the sheep-runs of Joseph's friends. He found them at nightfall, not in their customary open pasturage but in a more secret place of rock-clefts to which Joseph led him.

Nothing was spoken when he arrived among them. Enough was known of grief on either side and in the silence they prepared both for the affirmations of their prayer together and for the tragic psalm they were about to chant. When their worship was done, Elijah began to speak.

"You will tell me, you of the country about Jezreel, of more sorrow than I can relate. But Baal is again claiming his victims. Five prophets of God I saw slaughtered, even as their incense of praise was changed to the savour of mourning. Many more will die, perhaps we among them, before the stain of the Tyrian blasphemy is wiped from our soil.

"But we must not wantonly seek death; the honour due to God can be rendered as warmly and as worthily in the silence of your chamber or the austerity of a hillside as in the flourish of public worship. Your lives must be held precious – they are the sole weapons we men have, to maintain the right. Jezebel is perhaps an evil woman;" he paused as if to hold their own argument. "It may be that she is no more than a tragically mistaken creature, the victim of the inescapable fact that she was born Tyrian. There must be no mercy for the errors, though there may if God wills, be compassion for her self. The pity of God she may reject – I greatly fear she will – and she will certainly have no pity for her opponents. The struggle will be long and fearful and only God can tell the outcome.

"But one thing I have still to tell. For the years before

57

us, the natural world, sun and cloud, the dews from the chill of night, will be our weapons, our weapons *in their absence*. In all that time before us, there will be neither dew nor rain, the crops will fail, our beasts will die of thirst and man will be led to the brink of despair. *That* and that alone is God's opportunity, the destruction of the wanton idols and the place for penitence and the return to him and the ways of peace. It will require all your fortitude; thirst will be more terrible than hunger and you will plead for respite and *it will not come*. And then will come deliverance and we shall return to a land cleansed and again asking for rebirth."

There was a dark silence between them and they took to their rest.

In the morning Elijah took Joseph aside and to his astonishment and fear, told him of his intention to visit Jezreel before returning to Jordan.

"But why invite the danger you warned us of last night?"

"For Naboth."

"Naboth? No man is more secure, less in need of your supporting presence."

"No man is in greater danger. No sacrifice will be more tragic than his. We must have at least an hour together in the safety of dusk. We need make no foray into Jezreel, the city itself. If we skirt the hills, come from the south, we shall enter Naboth's domain without disturbing anyone about his home."

Joseph looked troubled, perhaps as concerned for his own and Naboth's safety if this disturbing man broke into their lives. Would Israel ever be rid of Elijah, that voice, that towering presence? He recognised the events that had dragged his intervention from the desert. At the same time he recognised the power of Elijah over him and submissively he set out to find the unusual approach to Jezreel.

58

They arrived as they had hoped in the lowering dusk. Elijah remained sheltered in the olive grove which surrounded the vineyard until Joseph returned to say that Naboth welcomed him.

Within the quiet chamber in which Naboth relaxed from his duties there was bread and wine waiting for the travellers and Naboth waited courteously for Elijah's words. He had heard much of this invasion from beyond Jordan, of the impact of his words upon Jezreel, indeed upon Israel. Word had reached him that even Jezebel had quailed, before again clinging to her purpose.

"Joseph has been persuading me that I should advise you to leave Jezreel. I shall not do that. I think your life would end if you were not in this place where all your ancestors have given their lives to the creation of your patrimony. But forgive me that I, a shepherd from the desert fringes, counsel you in the manage of your estate. I have prophesied – and it is the truth of God's word – that there will be years of drought, in which not even the dews of heaven will descend. Your vineyard will survive one year of such drought; after that, however skilful the tillage, nothing can save these acres of vines. And that is why I tell you that you must stay in this place. One year the vines will live, a second year with care – I cannot instruct you about mulching and hoeing! – the older, deep rooted vines will survive and you will know that no grapes must be allowed on the branches and even the branches themselves must be thinned without mercy. If the drought lasts a third year – and I cannot see the ways of God with Ahab and Jezebel lasting a shorter time – then all your skills will be needed to save a remnant.

"I think I know how I should work, for I have seen the near-failure even of oasis-tillage. Joseph, I feel sure, will sacrifice his young vineyard – it will take only a year or two to reestablish it to this young maturity –

and all his time must be devoted here. If my eye tells me truth, this deep soil hides springs that run in clefts of the underlying rocks. Dig deep, both you and Joseph and a workman or two, until, here, at the highest point of the vineyard, you strike a spring. Dig again, until along this ridge below your house, a line of deep springs will have been found. Grub up alternate lines of your mature vines and cover the soil about the others with deep layers of herbage – gather it in haste before the sun destroys life on the hill-sides – for even dead and rotted, this will be the salvation of your remainder vines. Then will come the labour. Dip sparingly into the wells you will have made and water those plants in need. You will be like slaves to your vines but by the mercy of God, the skeleton of your patrimony may be saved."

Joseph nodded his immediate understanding of Elijah's words and, with a silent misery, Naboth also assented.

"But there is more. The people of the city, their numbers swollen by the starving from the countryside, will be desperate in their thirst and hunger. Every gesture and speech from the royal palace will urge them to placate Baal and his underling gods and goddesses. Say nothing! Make no protest but in the quiet of your chamber here, or in the bitter silence of your labouring in the vineyard, commit yourselves to God; trust his ways, even though they may appear to be death. At least two men in Jezreel must be faithful."

There was little more to be said. Elijah could not risk another day in the environs of Jezreel and left before dawn to strike for Jordan after traversing the length of the valley. By nightfall he was on the bank of Jordan.

Elijah's family had had no word of him for all the weeks of his absence and his first care was to see them and bring reassurance of his health. Rumours only had reached Tishbe and they had lost little on their journey eastward. The cities of Samaria and Jezreel were alien in every way, as they pursued their frugal way on the desert margins and the women were eager to know the secrets of city life, its luxuries and excesses. But the men knew, even from Elijah's silences, that there were more than luxurious excesses to account for his sombre looks. He told them little of the persecutions and slaughters but asked their approval of his advice to Naboth; then, quietly and without exaggeration, he warned them that he would be a lodestone of trouble, perhaps of tragedy even in this remote place. He had said enough of the character of Jezebel and her dominance over Ahab and his court, to know that her enmity would be uncontrolled.

"I shall leave you tomorrow. If questioned you must admit that briefly you saw me and spoke with me. But I want you to be able to say with truth that you know nothing of my whereabouts; that you suppose me to be about some distant business and in no way in hiding. You may hint that to the best of your judgment from past years, I have probably sought the oases and then perhaps gone south to my nomad friends – but of course, you could be mistaken. It is a vast and cruel land to search and I hope they might soon tire."

It was clear to Elijah where he must go and with as much plain food, dry bread, with figs, raisins and olives, he made his way north to the valley of the Brook Kerith; in the cave-systems he already knew there would be safety and a morning climb to the ridge-crest would give him clear views to east and west, a sufficient time of warning of any pursuit. Carefully gathering small branches and a covering of leaves and grasses – for his time here might be long – his shelter was almost as

61

comfortable as home, his mantle an adequate covering for the cold of night.

And so the months passed, with no hint of pursuit. Autumn came and became winter. In neither direction did the winds of the late months offer snow or hail, for the skies remained cloudless in the depths of winter. With memory of his advice to Naboth, Elijah sought in the depth of the rock a spring which appeared to come from very deep in the limestone. He cleared it of the debris of autumn and set flat stones both below and above the trickle of water. Unless the very depths themselves failed, he seemed safe from the direst thirst.

Food was another matter. He was sparing, as the desert-dwellers had taught him. A handful of raisins or two or three dried figs seemed to suffice them for a day but there came a time when these were reaching their last. He had done what he could in gathering the few herbs which survived longest, until the drought defeated even their resistance. For another week he chewed on their stems and persuaded himself that they sufficed. But there came a day when he knew he could survive only a little longer.

That night he left his cave shelter and lay, wrapped in his mantle, on a shelf of rock outside its entrance. His sleep was troubled, for hunger gnawed at him even as he slept; and his dreams were troubled by the whirring of wings. When he awoke he saw the source of his dreaming, for, as he raised himself on his elbow, a single raven observed him from a higher rock before flying beyond the crags and when Elijah rose to look at the foot of the raven's ledge, there, scattered on the smooth rock were fragments of barley-cakes and a few small pieces of roasted meat. Slowly he ate them – desert dwellers would have deemed it a feast – and felt his strength return. Even the spring water tasted purer that morning and he spent the day gazing out over the

Jordan valley and trying to imagine the events of Ahab's kingdom. That night he lay down on his bare ledge, knowing that the food of that morning could preserve life for perhaps a week. His sleep was dreamless and he was awakened at dawn by a whirr of wings, as two ravens took their flight westward. At the foot of the crag his food was spread out for him, manna in this strange wilderness, and he blessed his ravens as though they were angels.

His first objective was the oasis beyond Tishbe. His own mind had become very clear in the months of solitary living in the crags. He knew the personal choices, the risks, and he felt he knew the next steps. But there was wisdom in the desert. His nomad friends had lived not months but years with the simplicities and he wished to test his experiences against their humble wisdom.

He made his way to the oasis nearest to Tishbe. He was wholly accustomed to a solitary stay there and he knew it would be at the very most a week or two before some of his friends came with their flocks. And so it was. They greeted him warmly, for they had heard disquieting news of his journey and his recent absence from Tishbe. That night, about the fire, he asked them for their advice.

"To me the issue is clear, Jezebel is not to be despised. She may be the instrument of evil; she may even endanger the life of our whole nation. But she is not despicable. There is a nobility in her bearing which brought to my mind the tradition of our fathers concerning Lucifer, Son of the Morning, who fell from glory. She has great beauty and has a power beyond that of men; Ahab is a child in her hands."

This quiet reflection was something they had not heard in Elijah's voice in their earlier friendship. This lean and fierce figure who paced about their encampment, had in his eyes a quality of contemplation as he spoke of conflict and danger, as though death had been more than matter for meditation; it had been faced, even endured in this new man they saw before them. The oldest among them replied to his unspoken question:

"All we hear of Jezebel and the matters of Jezreel makes us assume no compromise. You have already, we are told, declared the will of God: penitence or the merciless onset of drought. She will not start aside and I think you must prepare yourself for a wilder struggle. Your body is stripped for the contest, hardened beyond that even of our young men. But you will wrestle with no ordinary adversary. Have you calculated the power of Baal and Asherah, as they call upon those who worship them?"

"Idols have no power. Baal-Melqart is a child's tale, dreamt of on a dark night; Asherah is the dark growth of lust."

"That will not be Jezebel's opinion nor the faith of those she has gathered about her. The conflict will be as fierce as the loss they would suffer if God and the power of your arm prevail. When the battle is joined, never deceive yourself that you have mere dreams as adversaries. Take your rest now. There are no spies this side of Jordan and we can safely leave decision to the morning."

Elijah slept in the sure tranquillity of one who rested among friends. In the morning both he and his companions were clear. They summed up their thought with the warning, "Conflict will be fierce and until death;" his demands for himself had greater complexity.

"The great commanders, before they enter the field have one clear demand on themselves: 'Know your enemy.' Omri and his son Ahab have been such mighty warriors and I believe that Jezebel 'knows her adver-

64

sary;' in that one encounter of so few minutes, she read my mind and will with the clarity of a prophet – perhaps there was such simplicity to understand! But I had no such complete knowledge. You have heard me speak of her beauty – it would have unmanned me if my flesh had been made for that temptation. But there was more than beauty in her eyes and on her forehead; there was thought, resolution and anger and her speech had the controlled power that comes from a disciplined will. Now, in the quiet of these months of solitude, I have asked myself one question only: from what source is that will nourished and sustained? What power lies behind that seemingly fragile woman? Can it be possible that Baal-Melqart and Asherah kindle such devotion? Can fragile dreams engender that strength?"

"It is you, Elijah, who called them dreams; you spoke of them as though they were night-phantoms."

Elijah's mind shifted sharply under this challenge. "Moses brought to our people the Torah. In the ten words we hear with the force of unquestionable demands, 'Thou shalt', 'Thou shalt not.' Those words which began 'Thou shalt not', lead us to a number of sins which in one man would weigh down Lucifer in hell – 'not steal', 'not bear false witness', 'not commit adultery', 'not covet' and behind these words I hear a more terrible command: 'Thou shalt not hate the Lord thy God.'

The breath of his hearers was sharply indrawn, as though they feared the consequences of this uttered blasphemy. But Elijah was poised for struggle, as much with himself as with any external enemy.

"Can it be that in the depths of our being there sleep powers that demand this constant cry from Sinai, 'Thou shalt not'? Does Baal-Melqart make his dwelling in our hearts and minds, Asherah in our loins?"

There was a fearful withdrawing, as though Elijah's

65

mere words could carry pollution; but his pursuit of the truth he must find, pushed him relentlessly on.

"Last night, as I woke once to the brightness of the stars, it seemed to me, with the clarity of revelation, that there is only one way in which I can find my answer. Jezebel is out of her country; she is clouded for us in the threat she poses to God's way in our lives. If I am to know the true power of Baal and Asherah, I must know it in the lives of those who worship them of a free heart, with no desire to invade or conquer. I must know those who worship them with the certainty which I saw in those shepherd-prophets of the hills of Jezreel. Only then will God meet Baal in the depths of my mind and the field of my battle be defined."

"And this takes you where?"

"Tomorrow I leave for a long journey, to the coasts of Phoenicia beyond Tyre and Sidon."

His project was of such daring that it seemed to defy the forces and even the spies of Ahab and Jezebel. He once more crossed Jordan and, avoiding all inhabited places he traversed the hills above Beth-shan, not entering any of the valley of Jezreel which so attracted him. Taking the mountain route between Shunem and Nain, he rested on the hill-side, where, with sunset he saw the great plain of Samaria and at dawn saw the escarpment which led him to the heart of Galilee. Here his ridge-road was clear before him. One goal appeared to be Carmel and the next night he slept on its eastern slope but with morning he skirted the massive shoulder of land to see for the first time the waters of the Great Sea.

The sky above was merciless, as it had been for a year since his prophecy. The morning sun gave a startling sheen to the nearer waters, slightly rippled by the dawn breeze. But it was the immensity of the horizon which held Elijah in awe. From the height above Tishbe he was accustomed to looking into great distances, westward beyond Jordan to the great land masses even of Samaria; and if he looked eastward there were the near wilderness and the boundless sand of the desert. But neither of these vistas was uninterrupted; westward he would see the deep green of the Jordan valley, the parched ochres and light yellows of the wilderness and the wild contours of the central mountains. Even eastward there were the contrasts of wilderness and desert and, shimmering above the oases, those misty deceptions which led the traveller to look for lakes of water. All that his eyes had searched hitherto had the complexity of vast landscape which his eyes shaped into patterns of new creation.

But here was a different and disquieting prospect. Here was simple immensity and out of this vastness he could conjure no creation. In these waters were the mighty deeps. Here was the first gesture of creating Adonai, separating the waters above from the waters beneath. Here surely he was at the first day of creation and he an unbegotten alien. For the first time in his life he felt utter, unrelieved loneliness, that solitude of Adam on which God had compassion, bringing forth Eve. He tried to blot out the waste sea and looked northward. Before him there unfolded the plains of Phoenicia, no habitation visible at this distance and in the vaster distance in the north, no grateful terminus to his gaze in the cedars and snows of Lebanon.

His sense rebelled at mere immensity and there was borne in on his mind the first glimmer of thought, that if his forebears in the land of promise had had no more than the seas of Philistia to bound their gaze, they too, if God had not spoken to Moses, might have created a God, a Goddess, out of the depths of their longing. Did this begin to interpret Jezebel to him?

He threw the disquieting thought aside and descended

67

for a day to the plain. Here he saw that its emptiness had been the illusion of height, that there were hamlets at the sea-shore – he saw small craft and nets drying in the sun – and that the lower hillsides, seemed, in gentler months than these, to offer a richer pasture for the flock, than the meagre soil of upland Samaria. He took the path of a dry water-course, its mud deep-fissured by the months of drought and rested for the night in the shade of a mature juniper. He looked in vain for any of the berries which had sometimes in their bitter tang broken his thirst, but there was neither berry nor leaf among the thorns. His prophecy was all too completely fulfilled and its threat extended beyond Israel to neighbouring Phoenicia. The next day, passing between Aphek and the sea, he reached the hills above Acco but avoided the dwellings and kept his journey northward to the outskirts of Achzib and then turned inland to the mountains that embraced Abdon. For the first time since the heights of Carmel he was without sight of the sea and he breathed more freely in the wild contours of these hills.

The fascination of new experience drew him again towards the sea and for two days he walked north-westward along the fringes of the Phoenician hills. Below him he saw the buildings of another town and learnt from a passing countryman that this was Zarephath, the last town of consequence in northern Phoenicia. Elijah was reluctant to enter a city again and spent a day exploring the valleys which opened out into the plain of Zarephath. In late afternoon he saw, near a fringe of scrub, a woman gathering sticks in a field. She appeared bent by age and toil and appeared not to hear his approach, as she placed each fragment of wood in her gathered apron. When he was a few paces away from her she looked up and he saw a face in which the remains of young beauty still shone and though her eyes were clouded with extreme weariness, they were the eyes of a young woman. He stooped to the foot of the hedge and drew out a bigger gathering of branches, beyond her strength to carry.

"Your home?" She indicated a bank below the hedge and when they reached it, he saw a neat home, with the desolate remains of a garden which must once have been carefully tended. From the cottage came the thin wail like the first cry of a lamb and the woman stumbled to a run as she responded to the cry.

Elijah followed her to the door and saw her cradling in her arms a boy of some four years, feverish and wasted from thirst. Elijah spoke gently.

"Give me the child while you kindle the fire at your hearth. I too am hungry and the three of us must eat together."

"I have no more than a handful of meal left to us and a drop of oil at the bottom of the jar. I was about to prepare our last meal for my son and me and then compose ourselves for death."

"It will suffice and will not dwindle. You will not hunger in these months before you."

The woman in her weakness looked at Elijah listlessly, as though beyond the reach of hope but did as he asked. He built the fire of twigs as he would have done in an oasis and watched her as she mixed a cake of barley-meal and oil and placed it on a heated sheet of metal to bake. As Elijah sat before her and, parting the little loaf into three fragments, murmured a thanksgiving she looked startled into his eyes and, to his astonishment, murmured 'Amen.' He said nothing and they held silence while they ate, he gently touching the boy's hand as he persuaded him to take his portion.

The woman set the boy down to sleep in his cot and then they sat silently before the fire. At length Elijah said – it formed a question to challenge her:

"You whispered 'Amen.' "

"I am of your blood and faith, a worshipper of God."

"And living here in Phoenicia."

"My husband died three years ago and I have no strength to return to my kin in Samaria, so long as this drought lasts. He was a trader in fine cloths and thought that here in a post in northern Phoenicia there would be both a means of selling the materials he got from his homeland and also the opportunity to import from Cyprus, Cilicia and the land about Antioch. But Hebrew blood was hated in Phoenicia, no home could be found in Zarephath itself and at length we bought this little holding from a shepherd who seemed to understand our plight. Then little Samuel was born and then, as he began to run about our home, the drought descended. Each day my husband had gone into Zarephath to sell his remaining stock but he took a fever, a wasting illness and died. When the drought came upon us we had little to struggle against it, Samuel and I; you have come to see to our burial."

"No! to your life again and in Israel. But for these months, until you strengthen, we must wait here in a strange land."

Hannah took the child in her arms and went into the inner room to prepare for sleep. Elijah went to the shelter of the entrance-porch, wrapped himself in his mantle and slept.

The following morning he left before Hannah and the child were awake and spent the hours before noon in gathering more substantial wood for the fire than the twigs from the hedge. When he returned, Hannah was seated at the entrance, her arm about the child, Samuel.

"You are both happily named, Hannah and Samuel!"

"It was my husband's wish. He liked my name and at Samuel's birth, he thought that the prophet's name would be specially suited here, an alien land 'where there was no open vision.'" She smiled tentatively,

70

wondering whether, in the seeming austerity of Elijah, it would sound like the echo of a jest. Elijah's open smile reassured her and he said,

"We must eat; the fire is kindled for the barley cake."

"There is neither meal nor oil, for the last was used at our evening meal."

"Go to the vessels and see." He heard her astonished cry, as in both vessels there was sufficient food for all three. They broke bread in silence that noon, Samuel gazing in wonder at this powerful man, his fierce face breaking so readily into a smile. And so it was over the weeks – Elijah went each morning into the mountains, to return at noon, where a marvelling woman placed before them sufficient food for sustenance.

"It is always exactly enough" she said.

"As the manna always was each morning', he replied and no word was needed, of miracle or the providence of God.

There came an evening when the child was asleep, that Elijah felt that Hannah trusted him sufficiently to open her heart over her Phoenician neighbours. To his questions she replied,

"They are not an unkindly people. They are much wealthier as a nation than our kin of the Samarian highlands and yet the working-people are tempered and hardened by the variety of their toil. So many of them brave the storms of the Great Sea, whether in distant trade or in fishing along the coast, and many tend their sheep in these hills that enclose the city. Each trade is arduous and makes for a hardy people. Nor are the women idle. They keep happy households and their time spent away from children and the family food is spent with the wool, which they comb, spin and weave. Their skills with dyes was a marvel to my husband who craved their secrets but in vain. All he knew was that lichens, certain herbs and the bark of certain trees made

71

infusions which the woven wool drank readily. When, in the summer evenings they spread their dyed work over their near fields, the whole neighbourhood of their houses seemed like a dazzling pattern for a rare carpet and if the breezes came up from the sea, the cloths moved like a peasant dance of colour. What I think roused my husband's envy was that the patterns were never garish. You could scarcely even say that there was clear red, a blue, a green, for these living dyes, drawn from the plants about them had what he called 'broken colours' – red was always about to be the colour of an orange-rind, russet and brown were preferred to an unbroken blue or green, while the yellows had all the delicate variety of spring flowers in the wood clearings."

Elijah had not heard this animation in her voice since he first came to her home and he knew that life had begun to spring again. In the years before her, and returned to her kin, Hannah would find another husband who would stir her mind and heart to a similar joy in life.

Meanwhile he had knowledge to glean.

"You know something of their worship?"

"Very little." Once more she was tight-lipped and Elijah knew that he had to wait for her confidence.

"Some months before Samuel was born, one young woman, bolder than the rest, said to me, 'You must take gifts to the grove of Asherah; she alone can bless your womb.' I didn't understand her saying but one evening in the quiet autumn, we passed the grove and heard from within wild music and the screams of those who appeared in a frenzy. My husband hurried away and would say no more than 'this they call worship' and sadly took me to our home. Out of the silence later that night he said, 'They think of Baal as fire, lightning, the blasting of the thunderstorm and so – in their ignorance

72

– the blessing of their warriors and the bringer of victory. Asherah is a darker being, goddess of frenzy and out of the wildness, the throbbing notes of their music, they say that fruitfulness springs.' I know no more than that, for he would not speak of it again. Soon my hands were full and my mind satisfied with care of husband and my new child."

Elijah's courtesy forbade any questioning, and he had already learned all he could expect to learn in this visit to Phoenicia. He allowed the days to heal Hannah's spirit and quiet time to mature the growing boy.

One morning Elijah told Hannah that he would be away for two days and three nights, for he wanted to explore further into the hinterland. He set out eastward and soon found that he was faced, after the foothills, by a mountain mass greater than any he had compassed in Israel. High noon with the cloudless skies made movement in the precipitous crags difficult but he pushed on to the summit and there saw a landscape of great mountain masses stretching in every direction. Drought had given it a forbidding uniformity of tone and burnt texture; there was no stream or spring to give any animation to the land and Elijah soon tired of a sight which told him nothing of men and their lives in what might have been a country of prosperous husbandry with rich forest lands.

He descended directly towards Zarephath and hoped to be greeted as usual by the cries of Samuel's welcome but the house was silent, with no sign of Hannah or the child. As he approached the door he heard the sound of quiet sobbing and before the empty hearth he saw Hannah rocking the still body of her child and at the sight of Elijah breaking into more violent weeping.

73

"Samuel is dead! I have brought down on our heads the anger of Jahweh but why should innocence suffer?"

Elijah took the child from her arms and carried him into the inner room and laid him on the bed and loosened the folds of his clothes. He then stretched himself on the child, pressing hard into his breast and, laying his lips to the child's mouth, breathed gently into the parted lips. It seemed a long space before he felt the first warmth in the child's body and a flutter of indrawn breath. He continued to lend the child his own life and at length was able to stand at the side of the bed, gently chafing Samuel's hands and wrists. Within the hour he was able to raise the child to its feet and walk into the outer room, giving him to his mother. She held him close, threatening his breathing by the force of her embrace and he struggled to release himself.

"I have had a long sleep, mother," he said.

BOOK FOUR

Elijah retraced his steps towards Carmel, following the dusty sheep-paths along the hills and parallel to the Great Sea. His thoughts were a tumult, Jezebel and Hannah struggling for mastery. What possessed the one? What preserved the other in tranquillity when her world, so fragile in itself, was threatened by such forces without? Which would prevail in the destiny of Israel, fallen Eve and the seduction of Lilith, or Eve tried by fire and on the brink of redemption? It seemed to him, as he made his way in the cruel sun, that he, Elijah, was the field of battle, that the struggle had to be resolved in him.

Not seeing the way in his mind, he allowed the monotonous tread of his feet to take him towards Carmel. For the first time since leaving Tishbe, Kerith and his own people, he, the consecrated prophet, could see nothing of the way ahead.

It was an unkempt gathering at the court of Ahab. The king sat alone, bewildered as the messengers came before him to report their search for Elijah. Jezebel had commanded that her throne be set apart from the king's and she sat, seeming impassive, but her hunger blazing in her eyes.

The messengers had been commanded before Ahab, to proceed without ceremony. They stood in desperate weariness, their clothes worn and dishevelled, their bodies filthy as the sweat held the dust of the roads.

"No word of him?" Ahab's cry was incredulous and he looked at the dozen men before him, who had been chosen both for their strength of body and their loyalty to the royal house. Seven of them noble Israelites from the hill forts at the heart of Ahab's kingdom; five were athletic Phoenicians, passionately loyal to Jezebel and fired with her hatred for the miscreant prophet. If word there was of his actions and intentions for the future of Israel, surely these were the men to find the secret.

"The lands beyond Jordan, which spawns these men; what had his fellows to say?"

"Nothing, my lord."

"And Damascus? You scoured to the north; what had they to say?"

"Nothing, my lord."

"Beer-Sheba and the Negev; what more likely hiding-place; what had the nomad herdsmen to say?"

"No word, my lord."

"And the lands of Philistia, or the Phoenician shores of the Great Sea; would the fox have doubled towards an alien bolt-hole? What had their wisdom to say of his ways?"

"Nothing, my lord."

And so the wearying questions went on. To give them their meagre due, these young seekers had searched not only the kingdom but every land on its borders. Rulers, whether friendly or suspiciously hostile, had been called into service. Elijah, the menace of the kingdom had to be found. A single question, steely, but with voice scarcely raised, came from Jezebel, as the inquisition drew to its impotent close:

76

"You have not found the man, for all your seeking; but has there been *rumour* of him?"

One of the Phoenicians answered:

"Not one breath of rumour, O Queen, though we questioned closely. Some suffered under our questioning but no-one had seen trace of him, nor heard even the echo of his voice."

There was no more to be gained from prolonging the question and the twelve were dismissed to their usual duties.

Ahab, as the questioning had revealed nothing of the whereabouts of Elijah, had allowed other concerns, perhaps more immediate, to occupy his mind. Having dismissed his spies and risen to see Jezebel and her women to their quarters, he called Obadiah his chamberlain before him.

"We can find nothing of the intentions of Elijah. We cannot hope that he has died – there would have been some sign from men or the gods to tell us of such an event! – and we must assume some further disasters to tell us of his return. Meanwhile tragedy surrounds us. Our people starve as the land dies; even the court feeds less sumptuously – though some kings, our neighbours, have been generous – and our royal stables have seen consumed even the dusty remnants of straw. Soon our chariots and carriages will rust in the stalls.

"A greater scouring of the country must begin. The more astute in the uplands may have hoarded provender; the sheltered valleys of Galilee may still have springs and a little pasture. Seek, Obadiah. Take men and scour the country. Our horses and some of our people must survive."

"That is royal wisdom, and it may happen that in this humbler search, a quarry may start from his hiding; Queen Jezebel will rejoice at his capture."

Ahab looked suspiciously into the eyes of Obadiah

but there was no suggestion of hidden meaning, malice or innuendo in the bland smile of his chamberlain and he waved his dismissal. It would be disaster indeed, as great as the drought, if Jezebel were thought to have gathered the reins into her delicate hands.

Obadiah took with him only four men to assist in the search, three of the young and athletic courtiers and the heir of a wealthy farmer from the valley of Jezreel, a man already wise in the management of crops and the pasturing of herds and one who knew the astuteness of his country workers. No lie or prevarication would conceal a hoard from his quiet questioning.

They began their search north and westward, into the hinterland of Samaria and then bore directly north into the Galilean uplands. Here, as Ahab had supposed, the sheltered valleys had a minimal growth of grass and weed, wholly insufficient for man and beast on their land but yielding a little to the grasp of Obadiah. Small bales of fodder began to make their way to Jezreel.

Obadiah then looked towards Carmel, in a desperate hope that the high ravines might yield a little to their search. He was leading his party, weary and dispirited now from the weeks of searching and themselves desperate with hunger and thirst, when they were hailed by a voice from the top of the rock cleft up which they climbed.

"Obadiah! Stand, if you are wise! You hunt for food? or do you seek me? – a much more dangerous task!"

"We seek food and by chance have started our prey. We are five men in our full strength, Elijah, and we intend to take you before Ahab at Jezreel."

Laughter was rare among Elijah's emotions but his stride towards them mocked like laughter and there was irony in his tones, as he lifted his arms high above his head.

"Take me, Obadiah! Take me by your own strength

or the power of your lordlings. Have you chains to hold me, halters to lead me, as you marched towards Jezreel?" Through the matted beard and hair, the lean features drawn tight to the very bone, the nobility and power of Elijah still daunted his fellows and the five were no match for the strength of his will. As Obadiah hesitated, fearing to risk all if he commanded a rush to capture the prophet, Elijah spoke with authority:

"Go to Ahab in his palace. Command him – yes, Obadiah, command him in the name of God whom you once worshipped! – that he come to Carmel forthwith. I grant you all, you, your ministers, the king and all four hundred of the prophets of Baal, a week to prepare for your journey. In seven days from today you will all assemble at the broken shrine of God on this mountain; the shrine which Phoenician hands have polluted and which must now be cleansed with prayer, sacrifice and if need be, great violence. I see you hesitate! You have little time to waste – or is it fear of Jezebel, the alien harridan, that makes you pause?"

Even the insult failed to rouse them to any positive move and Elijah lashed them once more.

"Go, or your respite will reduce itself to hours."

They turned to the valleys of Galilee and made their best way towards Jezreel.

Carmel was like a teeming city. On the broad plateau at its summit was a smaller plateau, and sharp against the morning sky could be seen the jagged form of the shattered altar, little more than a group of standing stones. On the expanse of flat ground the four hundred prophets of Baal were drawn up in companies, formally facing the higher platform on which the single figure of Elijah could be seen, standing beside the largest of the altar-stones.

79

"King Ahab, I require word with you!"

There was a murmur of anger from the courtiers and the mass of people crowding below the ranks of the prophets, but none made any move against Elijah. Ahab stood with his nearest courtiers, Obadiah at his side and for an uncomfortable space, Ahab made no movement nor did his face show any of the conflict within. But generations had bred in him a reverence for prophecy and even a king must respect its command.

Slowly he made his way past the ranks of the prophets until Elijah's arm halted him some twenty paces below the altar of Jahweh, a distance sufficient to carry Elijah's voice beyond the king to those behind him who listened with fear for this meeting of powers.

"Ahab, I require that you make command, that here on this mountain your servants of Baal make an altar. With all ceremony and with what prayer they will they may build it and then with equal ceremony let them slaughter that calf they have brought, dismember it, placing it on their altar with the wood for kindling, and even incense, if they so wish.

"When they have done, and called upon their Baal, then we shall see what requires to be performed at the altar of God. For this is my challenge to you and your god: you say that Baal is a god of fire! Command then that he send down fire to consume your sacrifice. A god of fire has this drought to assist him! Call upon him, now!"

Rocks abounded in that place and under the eyes of Ahab, the prophets of Baal constructed their altar and with swift ceremony killed and parted the limbs of the calf, placing the sacrifice on the altar. In the deep silence of the people the prophets began their chant. At first it was little more than a low muttering, an almost silent memorial of the powers of Baal and all that he had done for the people of Phoenicia. Then the chant grew louder as the praises became articulate and the people of Samaria, who surrounded the ceremony, were appalled to hear the blasphemous degradation of the power of God as the prophets derided his name and cried the universal lordship of Baal.

Then came a great silence as the chant ceased and the oldest of the prophets stepped forward. On one sustained note the prayer rose before the altar.

"Baal, we cry to thee!"

The note died away as the prophets looked to the sky and then the cry was taken up by all,

"Baal, we cry to thee."

The chant rose frenziedly and then died away to silence. From the rock-platform above them came the mocking response.

"Baal's sleep is deep; cry louder!" The desperate chant rose again, the more piercing in the awed silence of the people below, and again it died away.

"Still he sleeps? Or perhaps on royal embassage to another god? or perhaps hunting on distant plains. He sleeps or is busy, this god of yours. Cry again!"

The frenzy now reached its height and the people saw the tragic ecstacy of the prophets as first one blade flashed and then another, as they cut arms, legs, torso and in their dance before the altar mingled their scattered blood with the blood of the sacrifice. But even ecstacy had an end and, exhausted, they fell to the ground.

There was silence throughout the heights of Carmel and into the silence the voice of Elijah. It had lost all mockery but his clear words carried to the furthest limits of the people below him.

"So, my people, you have seen the powers of Baal. Now, are there any faithful among you who will build the altar of Jahweh?"

81

As many leaped forward from the crowd below, Elijah raised his arm.

"No, my people. I need few arms to add to my strength. No stones need be sought, for here is the making of an altar, these stones torn apart by the heathen. In quiet and with prayer we will assemble them."

Four men joined him in the work and swiftly they gathered the stones together, building the altar in silence. The large slab for the sacrifice had been thrown aside but remained unbroken and again in silence the four men took it by its corners and placed it on the squared heap they had constructed. They stood aside as Elijah took a mattock and swiftly outlined a ditch about the altar. The men joined him in the digging and soon the stones were hemmed in by a ditch about a foot deep, with the soil thrown up, a rampart outside it.

An ox was brought before them and with ceremony it was killed, dismembered and placed upon the altar-stone. All was ready and the people, watched intently as the prophet, the altar and the sacrifice were outlined against the evening sky. They waited for the consuming of the offering and there was no sound as they gazed.

But for a while they were denied. A small group of serving men stood with waterpots at their feet at some little distance from the altar and Elijah waved them forward. He took one of the pots and holding it high in the sight of the people, poured the water over the beast of sacrifice. There was a gasp of protest from the people. This water would have slaked the awful thirst of them and their children. Quietly, with no look in their direction, Elijah took every one of the waterpots and emptied them until the altar and the ditch about it were drenched with water, already showing a steamy haze from the heat of the day.

Elijah stood behind the altar and in a clear voice addressed the people.

"How long will you halt between two opinions? If Baal be your god, follow him; if God be your god, follow and worship him. For you have seen the power of Baal, the God of Fire! I have had debate with our King Ahab. 'You are a troubler of Israel' he said to me as though it was my word, my command that brought this drought upon the land. My reply was just: '*You* are the troubler of Israel!' and he, even Ahab your king, had no reply to my accusation, which was the judgment of God most high.

"And now take note, O people of Israel. You have heard the prayers to Baal; listen now to the prayers offered to God."

Elijah drew near to the rim of the altar and in the tones of evening worship began his prayer:

> "Lord God of Abraham,
> Isaac and Israel,
> Show forth this day that thou art their God
> And the God of all Israel.
> And declare to this people
> That I am thy servant.
> Declare to thy people that all things
> Have been done according to thy word.
> Turn their hearts, O God,
> That their worship may be purified."

Out of the evening sky came a shaft as of lightning and struck the altar. Again and again it struck, until the sacrifice was burned and the water which had poured over the stones and which had filled the trench about the altar, was wholly consumed with the sacrifice.

Elijah stood silent at the purified altar which now stood in the sight of all the people. Ahab and his court prostrated themselves before the altar but the people were stirred to a renewed frenzy. The altar was purified but the land was still polluted. Taking their knives they rushed towards the prophets of Baal, who ran, seeking shelter among the defiles of Carmel's lower slopes. They were followed in their flight by the prophets of Asherah who had observed and guarded the ceremonies. But the people gained on them and at the foot of Carmel, in the dry water-course of the Brook Kishon, all the alien prophets were slain, their blood draining into the dust of the stream.

Carmel was a desolation. The people had gone to their homes and on the summit of the mountain two groups of men, separated, confronted as in seeming enmity. Near the altar of Jahweh two only could be seen, Elijah, seated on a rock, his head bowed in exhaustion between his knees; near him, standing in uncertainty as though waiting for a command, a young lad who in their last days had attached himself to Elijah as an unbidden servant.

Some distance below them was the chariot of Ahab and the tethered horses of a handful of his courtiers. Ahab was asleep in the chariot, fear and exhaustion had defeated him. The few courtiers who had remained with him, Obadiah among them, lay where they could find some place of rest. Over all was the silence that came from acknowledged defeat.

Elijah stirred and lowered his hands from his face. Around him were none of the signs of victory. He had commanded the slaughter, at least assented to its fierce completeness. For days in the merciless sun the stench of bodies would rise from Kishon. Birds of prey, gorged to their fill, would not suffice in all Carmel to rid the ground of this carnage. His mind sickened at the thought.

Was God also a God of Fire? How long would this contest last, devastating the hearts of Israel's people and destroying, polluting the very soil of their land. Silently he repeated the terrible declaration of God to his people:

'For I, the Lord thy God
Am a jealous God
And visit the sins of the fathers
Upon the children
Unto the third and fourth generation.'

The terror of this prediction drowned all thought and he looked wildly around for anything on which he could fix his thoughts, any action which would release the tension of his limbs. He looked long at the chariot of Ahab and foresaw no end to that conflict. Caught in the toils of an alien princess, far more powerful than he, what could Ahab do to redeem his manhood? A mighty warrior, there were no external battles to wage and the internal battle had already ended in his capitulation.

And Jezebel, what of her? Her powers were untested, for Ahab had tried only a tithe of her strength and conflict with Elijah had been almost entirely at a distance. Would it ever be engaged face to face?

But this day had been, above all, a distant defeat for Jezebel. The symbols of her power, the hundreds of Asherah's prophets, lay in the heaps of slain in the Brook Kishon and the non-existence of Baal had been shown to all people. Would Asherah fare likewise in their esteem? Jezebel was beyond calculation but it was a certainty in Elijah's mind that the death of a thousand prophets would be a trifling stumble in the progress of Jezebel towards her goal. Prayer to God, the strengthening of the hands and resolve of the shepherd-prophets of Samaria would be a labour that would stretch through the years until the death of Jezebel.

85

Meanwhile there remained the drought which threatened the extinction of his people. Was this also his responsibility? Had his words been true prophecy, declaring the will of God, or had there been a curse, carrying their consequences within their very sounds? He tried the words again on his lips.

"There shall not be dew nor rain these years but according to my words."

"To my words" – please God not "according to my *will*." It was not my will; if any will there was it was the will of God; my words were no more than the declaration of a future event." The words churned in his mind. 'A prophet' they had called him, a prophet with power. Could he be rid of this accursed vocation?

The young lad near him had fallen asleep, his head in the crook of his arm. Elijah looked with calculation at the sky and the height of the sun above the horizon. There would be another two hours of daylight and Elijah's restless thoughts demanded some kind of action, even action that appeared hopeless. He called the boy to him.

"Go to the crest of the hill and scan the horizon, if perhaps a cloud shows there."

The boy ran to the top of the hill and looked out over the sea.

"There is nothing." Elijah remained still, and after some minutes sent the boy again on the same errand.

"Still, master, there is nothing." Again and again he sent him and at the seventh time he ran back, panting in his excitement.

"Master! There is a cloud, though no bigger than the palm of your hand."

Elijah sprang up and cried aloud to Ahab.

"Set your horses within the chariot-harness and saddle those of your courtiers – and ride in haste lest you all be overwhelmed by the flood of water." And even as they were engaged in the harnessing, the whole sky above Carmel became black with clouds and as they touched the peaks, so the first rains poured on the hillsides. Elijah had seen no such rain and he took the frightened boy and hid him in his cloak.

The ravines were like streams in full winter-spate and the lower gullies were swept clean by the torrents of any of their earth and drought debris, so that even in the leaden light the cleared rocks shone as though burnished. Below Elijah, hands among the royal servants slipped on the leathers and thongs with which they fumbled at the harness for their flight. But at length all was ready and Ahab with his mounted guard began their precarious descent from Carmel.

Elijah watched their sliding progress and wondered if they would get to the plain before the gathering torrents made progress impossible. He hurriedly told the boy to run in the opposite direction and, avoiding the landward slopes of Carmel, make for his home on the coastal plain.

The scene of Elijah's contest with the prophet of Baal was already greatly changed, washed clean of superficial pollution in the torrential storm. Below, the dry bed of Kishon was now brimful, the slain men drowned in the deluge which streamed through the channel, a torrent as much blood as water. Yet, for all the devastation, one token remained there before his eyes, the altar of God, its fire and sacrifice washed away and the stones – twelve for the tribes who followed the most high God – washed as though new-created, a monument to steadfastness, requiring now no blood-sacrifice.

He saw that Ahab was ready for the journey and he ran to the side of the leading horse, grasping its rein and dragging its head to point in the safest direction for flight. The cavalcade gained speed and still Elijah ran along-side, grasping the leading-rein and avoiding both boulders and quagmires as they threatened Ahab's progress, a progress which every moment more ressembled flight than a return to a royal home.

At length they were on level ground, for Elijah had drawn them down to the Esdraelon road and from that clear way they could make passage to the valley and upwards to Jezreel.

The leading-rein was no longer needed as the horses took heart from the quiet of the night and the refreshment of rain. Elijah stood aside, tucked the skirts of his tunic into his girdle and gave himself to the swinging stride of the mountain-dweller, keeping comfortably ahead of the chariot of Ahab. By dawn they were at the gates of Jezreel and Elijah turned aside from the way into the city, went secretly into the garden of Joseph's house, beside the vineyard of Naboth and, waking his friend, asked his guidance to the place of sanctuary where he might find his shepherd-prophets.

The rains had now reached Jezreel and Joseph looked with pride beyond the sheltering olive-trees to the lines of vine, so carefully tended during the years of drought. They looked in good heart and would drink these first rains thirstily. He turned to Elijah with a smile:

"A year and they will be bearing as before. The wine will be good after our long thirst;" and they set out for the hills.

"Not one prophet spared?" Jezebel's anger blazed like a fire long smothered but she kept control of herself; anger should be a weapon and not turned upon herself.

"And you failed to keep Elijah at your side!" Ahab had done his best with the disastrous narrative; but there was no disguising the impotence of Baal and his followers and it was no consolation to Jezebel that Asherah had not been invoked but her prophets mur-

dered with Baal's retinue. The immediate need was
Elijah captive and made to pay for his iniquities. It
would be good to hear what, under torture, he confessed
of the means – the spells, the witchcraft? – by which he
had tricked the prophets of Baal, to know what device
had brought that consuming fire. She called her swiftest
and most trusted messenger and instructed him:

"Elijah will be somewhere in the rock-fastnesses above
Jezreel. Seek him out and tell him, from Jezebel his
queen: 'You have slain my servants the prophets; God
do the like to me and more, if by the morrow your life
be not as one of these.' Go, and having said your message,
return that we may send to the place you find and bring
him securely bound to Jezreel."

Elijah had gathered some half dozen of the shepherd-
prophets about him and soberly recounted to them the
events of the three-year gap in their friendship: of
Tishbe and Kerith; of Zarephath and of Hannah and
her son; of Carmel and the contest of altars and gods;
and of the abundance of rain and the swift journey to
Jezreel.

There was a sober pleasure in the telling and perhaps
even greater pleasure in the hearing. They were about
to recite together their evening psalm – it would be a
psalm of thanksgiving this night, for the infinite mercies
of God and his compassionate ways with men – when
the crag above them became the sounding-board for a
cry from the cleft below their rock-shelter.

"Elijah the Tishbite! Do you hear me, Tishbite? Do
you hear me? Jezebel your queen sends you a message;
give careful heed to it. You have slain the prophets; she
vows that she will die even as they are dead, if by the
morrow you are not as they are, cut off from the living!
Fare you well, Tishbite. We shall meet once more."

The arrogant voice was silent and Elijah looked at
his companions. The eldest of them spoke.

"It is no idle boast, Elijah. She has power still and her sword will be honed to a sharper edge by anger at your latest actions. There is no safety in these hills nor indeed in all Samaria. North to Galilee is to undertake a journey in populous places, whose people may not cherish a wandering prophet. She will expect you to cross Jordan, to be among your own people and the nomads who will shelter you in their wanderings. Let her servants search there but do you go south to the Negev. In those wastes, even if it is her will to search, she will scarcely find you."

They waited not even for deep night but sent Elijah on his way, eastward at first to the wilderness which separated them from Jordan and then south until he entered the environs of Beersheba. He avoided the dwellings and went on into the desert and, weary from his many days' flight, lay down in a sandy hollow beneath a juniper.

BOOK FIVE

Elijah woke to such a dawn as the desert sometimes grants. The sun was not yet above the horizon and the early flush on the eastern sky was giving way to gold as a few bars of low cloud caught the rays of light. He stirred restlessly, for his limbs had stiffened during the long sleep of exhaustion and he was reluctant to move from his cramped position. Years of privation, the conflict on Carmel and the successive flights to and from Jezreel were now taking their toll of his body.

Slowly he grasped his new situation, solitary in a strange part of the country, without friends and with no clear plan for the immediate future. He realised that the struggle with the house of Ahab would have to be resumed but for the time he needed seclusion to recover strength both for his body and his purpose.

Lethargy which now overtook him was hitherto outside his experience. From boyhood he had expected nothing but labour and hardship from life and certainly his 'Voice' had driven him further into deserts of the mind. He had never been a contemplative; nothing, no-one in Tishbe had led him beyond the simplest speculation and Torah, the history of Abraham and his heirs and the psalms of David had sufficiently nurtured a mind unused to abstraction. Now his life had been pierced by unaccustomed choices. God was not the only divine being demanding allegiance and worship, even if his soul revolted from granting his rivals any true reality. He had heard with wonder of the fall of Samson, of idols drawn into the life of Israel from heathen Philistia but these had been tales of long ago and there was sufficient wonder in the divine strength of Samson, the glory of the Nazarite vows, to overthrow the acrid taste of the philistine woman's seductions.

But as he thought back to childhood, he knew that Delilah would not fade from his mind. Those blades in her hand, the shearing of Samson's hair, the destruction of the vowed austerity – was this the permanent history of man, from Eve's compassing of Adam's fall to the menace of Jezebel? The conflict had been compassable so long as it was history; now the menace was alive and at his back; Jezreel no insuperable distance from Beersheba.

In his youth he had known weariness; in these past years he had experienced a total exhaustion; but never had be known even the shadow of despair. Fear in the past had been a spur to action and when the critical moment came, as it had on Carmel, then his courage had responded, sure in the reliance on human strength and divine guidance. But now despair grasped at him, in the weakness of his flesh and the exhaustion of his spirit. His 'Voice' was silent, giving no indication of the way forward, or the courage to return to the inevitable struggle.

Now also a new paralysis struck at him: there was no compulsion to the morning praise, no desire for the cry of his people, 'Hear, O Israel' and the psalms were silent in his memory. He could call up not even the echoes of the shepherd-psalm, for what relevance had 'still waters' in this desolation of sand?

The only prayer that remained was for death and Elijah murmured into the stillness:

"It is enough! Lord, now take away my life. For I am not better than my fathers, who suffered and died. Lord! It is enough; now let me die."

The cry was the more bitter in that the last years, since he had left Tishbe, now seemed vain. Nothing had been accomplished and the evil against which he had cried was as powerful as ever and would prevail. In the exhaustion of his spirit he drowned in sleep.

The sun was westerly when he awoke to the gentle stirring of his mantle. Near him, and smiling, as he saw him awake, was a tall figure who spoke simply and in words which struck away his lethargy:

"I am sent by God. Here is warm bread, fresh from the coals and a flask of water, fresh from the spring. Eat and drink and renew your strength."

Elijah did as he was commanded and, in the refreshment of his body, rested and slept, untroubled by dreams. Again there was the gentle touch at his mantle.

"Your sleep has been long and sufficient. Here again is bread and pure water. Eat and drink, and go your way as your spirit will command you."

Instinctively Elijah went south, putting still greater distance between him and Jezreel, traversed the barren Negev and then followed the stony way between the Wilderness of Shur and the western slopes of Sinai. Many days of rough walking, struggling from oasis to oasis, brought him south of the main heights of Sinai and memory of childhood narrative took him to the east. For now names became reality as he knew that he was in the steps of Moses and heroic struggle of old time gave meaning to his blind groping towards the springs of his vision, the source of his 'Voice.'

The journey was hard and made the harder as his fears drove him aside into shelter when he heard the sounds of travellers and their beasts on their way to trade in Egypt. But one late afternoon, very near to exhaustion; he saw the shadow of an oasis ahead of him. It was more extensive than any he had seen since he left the Wilderness of Shur and he hoped for shade, water and the fresh fruit of the date palm.

He entered the oasis and found a small stream flowing away from a well-head. He dipped his palm and tasted the brackish, salt flavour of water unfit to drink. Again bitter memory came to him – the Waters of Marah! But the date-palms were kinder and the fruit, fleshy in their near-ripeness, gave him, before sleep, the illusion of food and drink. The following morning he saw before him yet more hardship and memory of his forefathers told him that if he was to reach Sinai – his goal in these last days – he must now endure the Wilderness of Sin. For three days he struggled on, the yellow sand at his feet becoming darker, to a rusty brown as the lower slopes of Sinai weathered to this rougher sand and gravel. Soon, through gorges and the occasional ampler valley, he was led into the massive wilderness of rock, its crags towering above him with greater grandeur than he had known even on Carmel. Giants had carved these massive pinnacles! He smiled at the absurd fancy, and yet there was a superhuman quality, a menacing grandeur in these crowded peaks which was beyond the natural, beyond even the most menacing lands he had hitherto known.

Then his ascent led him into a broad cleft in the rock. The warm sandstone – familiar to him from the wilderness heights of Judah – now gave way to the harder granite. This too was red and in the clean fissures were the gleams of minerals for which Elijah had no names. Here the shapes were cleaner, more sharp in their fractures, for this granite yielded to no erosion from rain, like the lower sandstone, but broke under the alternate blows of sun and frost. One or two of the larger fragments held him with something approaching pleasure in their form but he knew that the summit demanded his ascent and evening saw him reach the height. Sinai was his, but his alone. No shade or echo of Moses broke the utter solitude of this peak.

He sought and found a small cave just below the summit. Had Moses rested here? was this the place where the surer voice which directed Moses had been heard, in words that echoed down the years for all Israel? In the warmth of this fancy, he folded his mantle as a pillow and fell asleep.

The morning was clear and in the early light he could see the reason for the secure silence in which he had slept. The cleft which had opened into his cave took a sharp turn above its entrance and again doubled back upon itself before opening out into the plateau which was the summit of Sinai. The passage to the cave, in its tortuous bending, broke even the gentlest breeze and its silence was a deep refreshment.

But with this goal accomplished, what remained to be done? Israel would scarcely benefit from his hiding here on Sinai. The House of Omri would continue its fatal reign and Jezebel again establish the dominance of alien gods. Nor was his solitary sojourn there even possible; starvation would drive him away from this shelter before the turn of a season. Once more the despair of Beer-sheba descended on him and turned sleep to nightmare.

He awoke into the still night. He walked to the summit and sat on a boulder, looking to the eastern horizon. As the grey clouds flushed to their first radiance, Elijah felt the stirring of a new hope and knew that his 'Voice' was about to speak.

"Why are you here, Elijah?" The direct question cut through the confusion of the last weeks and his journey to Horeb and Sinai. All the frustration and despair

95

which had marked the last stages of his journey, gathered into one bitter accusation of his people:

> "I have been very jealous for the Lord,
> For the Lord God of Hosts;
> For the children of Israel, thy people,
> Have forsaken thy covenant,
> Thrown down thine altars,
> Slain thy prophets with the sword.
> And I, even I, only am left.
> And they seek my life,
> They seek my life
> To take it away.
> It is enough;
> Lord, now take away my life,
> For I am not better than my fathers."

Was his life to end here, where Moses had scarcely begun the long desert march? Was there to be no peace, no reward for all the struggle with his Lord's enemies?

In the silence there was a stirring in the air about him and the words came clearly:

"Stand forth, Elijah and wait upon my words."

And the breeze of dawning grew to a mighty wind, which forced Elijah into a break in the rock. And as he cowered there, the wind grew to a storm, to a tempest, in which the very rocks were clashed together and fragments rained about Elijah's feet. There followed a silence as profound as the storm had been violent and Elijah waited for the word of the Lord. But the silence was unbroken.

As he waited, the rock against which he stood began to stir and he saw the pinnacles about him grind together as an earthquake shook all Sinai. The granite slabs clashed with a sound like metal and the ground at his feet heaved as if a sea had become rock stirred by a tempest. And the storm also was stilled and Elijah prayed in the silence that he might hear the voice of God. But again the silence prevailed.

Elijah moved from the shallow sanctuary in which he stood and began to move towards the cave where he hoped for greater safety. He had not left the plateau when a shaft of lightning struck one of the pinnacles and lightning continued to play between them, as though some force was weaving a net of fire about these peaks. And below him, where the earthquake had shattered the greatest of the rock-slabs, a pillar of sulphurous smoke rose from the fissure and as it dispersed about him, a tongue of flame leaped from the molten rock which poured from the opening and ran over the path below him, along which he had climbed to the summit. Still the lightning continued to weave the peaks in a skein of fire and still the flames of earth leaped to join the shafts above. Again Elijah cowered in his shelter, praying that the tumult would cease. It died away; the molten rock began to crust over and harden, losing its vivid red and orange and cooling to the grey of ashes. Above him the peaks ceased to ring with the lightning assault and there was silence again on Sinai. Surely after this tumult word would come.

As Elijah waited and still felt beneath his feet the faint stirrings of a troubled earth, Sinai became changed in his inner sight to the slopes of Carmel. The rocks of Horeb seemed to him to be the altar rebuilt on that gentler mountain and he heard his voice again demand fire of the Lord, a shaft that would consume the offering. And it had come; Jahweh had answered in the devouring flame. And again he heard his voice in its terrible command, "Kill and do not spare!" and the headlong flight of the false prophets ended in a river of blood. As he looked at that conclusion of his mission and heard the echoes of his own voice, he waited again. Twice

97

before there had been silence; surely now the God of Fire would speak to his prophet and the mission be sanctified, even spared to a greater effort.

But for the third time, as with tempest and earthquake, so with fire, the issue was a profound silence.

Elijah fell to the ground and remained in another agony of despair. His life was null, his hope for Israel denied and all his actions had been no more than the vain shattering of earth; the longing for death was overwhelming.

For hours he lay there and as the air about him became pure and still towards evening and the rocks had settled to their customary firmness, Elijah began to hear a whispering, little more than the murmur of a breeze. As he raised his head, the whisper became a still, small voice, gently audible as it repeated words he had heard before the turmoil.

"Elijah, Elijah! Why are you here on Sinai?" In his helplessness, Elijah could make no new reply but repeated fragments of his former chant before the God he worshipped:

> "I have been very jealous for the Lord,
> The Lord God of Hosts.
> I, even I only am left,
> And they seek my life.
> Lord, let me die!"

And still the voice returned, scarcely above a whisper but with all authority.

"Elijah! Stand and look about you. North, east and west, I have my people, seven thousand faithful who have not bowed their knees to Baal.

"And now I have labours for you once more. Travel north, even to Damascus and there you shall anoint Hazael to be king of Syria. And you shall return to

Samaria and there anoint Jehu the son of Nimshi to be king of Israel.

"And as your labours draw to their end you shall go among the gentle prophets of Israel and from among them choose one to be your heir, Elisha the son of Shapher of Abel-meholah, for my work will neither cease nor fail."

Elijah rested a few days after the storms of Sinai and then went a new way north to answer the commands of Jahweh. Descending the eastern slopes of Horeb, at length he reached Ezion-geber and made for highlands east of the Dead Sea and the valley of Jordan. It was a long and arduous journey of many solitary months and he had time to meditate on the revelations of Sinai. He seemed in his loneliness to have lost the God who had dominated his life since childhood, the Lord who demanded all his hardihood and who demanded sacrifice of him and death for his enemies. The new God who grew in his mind was of more tender command, requiring less heroic action of his prophet. All that Tishbe, Kerith and the harsh uplands of Samaria had bred in him, was all this now to be set aside?

He kept away from highways, for he had no desire for company as his thoughts revolved about this new vision of divine calling. As he entered the mountains of Moab, he saw deep below him the strange waters of the Dead Sea and the ghost-sculptures of salt on both shores. Some powers appeared to demand graven images, whatever the prohibition of Jahweh!

At length the highways were unavoidable as they converged on Kir-haresath, the capital city of Moab and there he submitted to his weariness and, at the northern limits of the town, asked for lodging and food, always given readily to a wandering prophet, and there set aside the rustiness of his tongue. As he spoke to his host and his family, he realised that months had passed without his exchanging a word with any human being. He found his own humanity coursing back and there was the beginning of the answer to his questioning the will of God.

He resumed his journey north in a greater quiet but again his mind was assailed by questions. For there, after a few days of journeying, was Mount Nebo, the height from which Moses had had his dying glimpse of the land which Jahweh had promised to his people. Sinai to Nebo – all unaware either that he had traced the way of Moses, or of the irony in this conjunction of mountain peaks, – he walked to the eastern slope of Nebo. He stayed there, undecided. He wished to follow the path to the summit, to see the land which his people had conquered. At the same time he was held by fear. Why should he trespass on this place of dereliction, where Moses had died, deprived of the fulfilment of his vision, that his people should be led by him from slavery to plenty? Questions came insistently to plague his half-resolved mind. Why had Moses suffered this tragedy? Was there cause in his history which merited this end, an unknown grave in alien territory?

As he had, many weeks before, entered the foothills of Sinai, Elijah had tested the truth of a story heard in childhood. The people of Israel, suffering from thirst in the desert, had begged Moses to find them water. God had told him to strike a rock once and he would find a spring gush out, sufficient to slake their thirst. Moses, angry at their constant complaints, had struck the rock *three times*. Water indeed gushed out in sufficient quantities but Moses was to suffer for his impatience. For his failure to heed God's command that he should strike *once*, he would lead his people to the entrance of their new land but would himself not enter, seeing it only from a distance and then to die and to have no known tomb.

Elijah had reached a similar place on the road to Sinai and, seeing a steep rock-fall at the side of his road, had raised his staff and struck at the rock. Its surface cracked and out streamed the water which had evidently been stored behind a skin of rock, to be released at a blow, whether from Moses or Elijah.

The incident had left Elijah obscurely troubled and his bewilderment returned as he looked upward to the slopes of Nebo. To strike a rock *once* or *thrice*? Was the offence so heinous? Had Moses, carrying the burden of a nation's safety, and no less human than the most weary of those he led, had he no right to feel impatience with his malcontent people? And further questions asserted themselves which bore heavily on Elijah's mind. Was prophecy so sure an insight? Could he, Elijah, or Moses before him be so sure of God's intention, that it could never be misunderstood in its smallest detail? Once or thrice? Was the command so meticulous and had obedience to it to be equally scrupulous?

And yet there was one further question. He had heard in his earlier years, as he grew – or so he supposed – into the prophetic calling, that all prophecy was declared in a modest formula: 'Thus saith the Lord.' There was no question that the great man should cry, 'Thus saith Moses – Aaron – Samuel – or Elijah.' The prophet was an instrument, a proclaiming trumpet at the mouth of Jahweh. And so, *once – thrice –* was Moses so surely culpable that he must bear this cruel dereliction, the denial of the fruit of labour which had torn at his life for forty years?

Somehow, in face of these questions, Elijah turned away sorrowing from the slopes of Nebo. Not for him the repetition of Moses's vision, the strained look over

101

the borders of Israel, the attempt to pierce the rich secrets of a land not yet possessed.

The weeks passed as he continued his northward way and still the questions turned his mind to turmoil and at length became focussed in one question only: was he, Elijah, to know the same fate? What was the meaning of that command that he should choose Elisha to be his heir in prophecy? Was the end so near for him, and his work but half done?

The contours of the hills were becoming familiar and his steps became firmer as he approached an oasis some two days journey from Tishbe. As he neared it, he saw that he would not be alone for the evening meal and the rest he craved. Greeting the nomads at some distance his joy was great to hear the answering hail, "Elijah!" His friends seemed never to fail him in his need and that evening about the embers which focussed their quiet talk, he told them of all that had happened to him since he left them for his assault on Jezreel.

The very telling was a purgation of spirit and before he went to his rest, his old friend said much that he had longed to hear, and fragments of his speech echoed in Elijah's ears as sleep overtook him:

"It has all been the will of God ... You have been much blessed in the strength of his right arm ... Soon you may take your rest, your life fulfilled."

Elijah spared himself only a day or two at Tishbe, passed over the lower waters of the Brook Kerith and, still keeping to eastward of the Jordan valley, crossed into the borders of Galilee and to the southern extremity of the waters of Kinnereth, that Sea of Galilee of which he had hitherto seen nothing. He avoided its western shores and kept to the heights of Gadara, keeping steadfastly north until he had crossed the mountains of Golan and reached Syria.

It was a secret matter to search out Hazael to be

anointed king of Syria and Elijah was dependent on his prophet's mantle and staff to preserve his safety, as he searched for the man. When he was found, it was secretly in a wilderness fastness that Elijah performed the ceremony, pouring the oil and pronouncing the intention of God – and immediately, once more to the road south, to seek out Jehu the son of Nimshi.

BOOK SIX

Elijah was not an old man. Through all the hardships endured, his years were not yet beyond 'middle-age.' Yet, as his friends spoke with him, he appeared to have reached an autumnal serenity. No more the barbed tongue, the flashes of destructive anger. Words were few and any answer long considered before the wisdom came.

Had Elijah been questioned, he could have said at what time the change had come upon him. Jahweh had given three commands: Hazael for Syria, Jehu for Israel and Elisha for himself. There had been fear and furtiveness in seeking out Hazael; there had been questions in his choice of the impetuous Jehu for his anointing and when it was done, Elijah sought the quiet places in the wilderness by Jordan.

Then solitude brought renewed questions. The 'seven thousand' of whom Jahweh had spoken; who were they and where did they live in safety? He was not far from Abel-Meholah where Elisha had been promised him as a helpmate and heir. As he retreated from the wilderness and went towards the town, the land became kinder and more fertile. Outside Abel-Meholah a large field was being ploughed, twelve yoke of oxen drawing ploughs in parallel ridges along the length of the land. One of the teams kept a few paces behind the others, the eleven keeping rank with care as they went, and responding to the command of him who ploughed to their rear. They were approaching the lower limit of the field and the twelfth ploughman held his ground, allowing the eleven to swing around him in a great half-circle until they were parallel to the first furrows and ready for the return along the length of the field.

Elijah watched with pleasure as the earth turned sweetly in the furrows. These were no crude plough-shares, merely to scrape the surface, but curved iron blades such as this soil deserved. Elijah murmured to himself, "This ploughing is 'fleet,' " for he saw that the ploughshares were so adjusted that they did not dig deep but turned only a hands-breadth of the sward; and he knew that the soil was rich and deep and that roots would strike down without too great disturbance of its texture. He looked with increased interest at the young man capable of directing this skilful work. His intuition told him that this was indeed Elisha and he waited as the twelve yoke of oxen trudged the full length of the field and were about to make their turn. The young man looked at him with a smile, as though welcoming him to an appreciation of their craft, and Elijah ventured to respond.

"Elisha!"

The young man's smile became broader as he replied, 'Yes, master?"

Elijah beckoned him over and took the mantle from his shoulders and threw it over the shoulders of Elisha, in the traditional ceremony of adoption. His response was a tentative recognition, "Elijah?" and, at the prophets' assent, he said eagerly.

"Let me make my farewell to my father and my family and I will follow you wherever Jahweh wills."

"Why should I disturb your life and your affections?

106

Go to your family and when they give you leave, then follow me."

That night the two men left the rich cultivated land and made for the wilderness. There, in the stillness, Elijah told him of the happenings on Sinai and the command of the Lord God and in Elisha's gentle features he saw complete understanding and assent to the way ahead. Those were the hours when the tranquillity of autumn came to compose Elijah's spirit.

So many months had passed since the threats of Jezebel that Elijah felt a longing to see Naboth and his neighbour Joseph once more. As they walked towards the valley of Jezreel, Elijah told Elisha of the friendship between those two men, so diverse in age.

"I am eager to see how the vineyard of Naboth has progressed and whether the sacrifice of Joseph in giving up his holding during the drought, in order to secure water for Naboth's vines, had now been rewarded."

Elisha told his master of the straits to which farmers had been reduced during the three years of suffering, and the measures they devised to see that there was not total loss of their land. He smiled his appreciation of Elijah's wisdom in advising Naboth to seek for water below ground when the rains failed.

"We tried to have a well of sorts in every large field, partly to be sure that our stock did not suffer extremes of thirst but also to water the most precious of our trees. It was beyond our hope to plough, sow and reap so long as the rains failed and we were sorely tried as we attempted to stave off hunger. Many a child died in that tragic time and many who survived will have no great strength to meet their later lives."

Elijah allowed him his brooding silence knowing that

compassion would be his greatest blessing when the inevitable struggle was renewed with the house of Omri.

Elisha could not long be kept from the details of husbandry.

"How deep had Joseph to dig before a stream of water could be found."

Elijah reminded him that he was a fugitive in those early days of drought and had had to flee after making his suggestions to Naboth and Joseph. Elisha might find matter of great interest in seeing both their labours and the results in saving the vines, if that had indeed been possible.

"We abandon our search for water too soon, thinking that we have dug in the wrong places. Whenever we know that beds of limestone lie beneath our land, there it is likely that streams of pure water will be found. It is often hard and dangerous work to dig so deep, but with water, so much more of this land would bloom and so many hungry people receive more ample food."

He brooded awhile on this failure of his people and then turned eagerly once more to Elijah.

"If only they would attend to the hints of our fore-fathers! Whenever you hear tell of water drawn up from a 'Jacob's Well', there you will see the wisdom and the patience of our fathers, for many of those wells are broad and deep and must have needed the patient toil of weeks – while the wandering cattle lowed and the sheep bleated, waiting for the saving water." He smiled with the assurance of one whose family had tested and trusted to the ancient ways.

"I think if we probed those wells of Jacob, we should find that, shallow or deep, they had struck bed-rock and that water never failed them, even in the depth of drought."

This was the first time that Elijah had known the continuous companionship of one he could trust. Even

108

the friends at the borders of Tishbe and Kerith had been wanderers, seen at long intervals and even the long stay at Zarephath had been with one whose lot was too hard for conversation. Now his spirit expanded in the new fellowship and he knew that though leaves withered and fell in autumn, autumnal warmth was the most gracious of the whole year.

As they ascended the valley of Jezreel, talk had to be rarer and in quiet. Elisha was curious to see this new and rich ground and exclaimed at the numbers of cattle, the variety of fruits and the promise of abundant grain. Once more Elijah decided on an evening approach to Jezreel, avoiding the ways to the city-gate and looking for entrance to the little domain of Joseph.

He found him resting in the last light of evening and looking out to the pale eastern sky. His exclamation as he saw Elijah before him was welcome enough and it was clear that the sight of Elisha, with the assurance of strength for Elijah, also gladdened him. After he had made his guests comfortable, he asked Elijah whether he should invite Naboth to join them at their meal.

"Indeed, yes. Only so will I get all the details of your history and Elisha learn the secrets of other ways with the land!"

Naboth came at once and it was obvious to Elijah that the years had not dealt generously with him. He had aged far more than the years since Elijah last saw him and, from the affectionate trust with which he looked at Joseph, it was clear that it was not his vineyard that troubled him. After their first greetings he became quite silent and Elijah felt impelled to ask him directly what troubled him.

"The drought had no sooner ceased than we, who loved Jahweh and his ways with men, saw that the chastening of the years had left no mark on Ahab. His fear of Jezebel and her demands was greater than his

109

fear of the Lord God of Israel. Their hands were raised as violently as ever against those with whom they were displeased. No! (he responded immediately to the unhappy questioning in Elijah's eyes) I have been untroubled except in mind. My humble wealth and the esteem of my fellows in this valley have kept me safe and I trust will continue to do so.

"But we are all too near that terrible grove. On Carmel, at the Brook Kishon, all the prophets of Baal and Asherah died. But it was a scourge too light for Jezebel. Few weeks were passed before they came by tens and by hundreds from the shores of Phoenicia; nightly we hear the singing, the laughter and the cries to Baal. It would seem as if Carmel had never been."

All three were silent as they saw the noble face before them furrowed in his desperation. Physical danger and privation had seemingly left his body untouched but his mind and spirit suffered beyond anything he had known in Israel.

Elijah saw that Elisha was moved to deflect these broodings. Turning to Joseph he said:

"Elijah tells me of the advice he gave you, as he prepared to flee from Jezebel's wrath. I have told him of the desperate measures we took at Abel-meholah to save what we could of our livelihood; did you fare as well?"

Joseph was relieved to pursue this topic and immediately drew Naboth into talk.

"It was no great decision to abandon my little plot and its row of vines. I knew that if we could save Naboth's stock, my land could readily be replenished when the drought was over. But that was a cruel task!

"First we knew that half the vines on my ground had also to be sacrificed." Naboth broke in with the countryman's concern for the welfare of the land.

"We pruned those that were left, far more stringently

than was our custom – we no longer hoped for grape-harvest – and we did our best, with the leaves and branches of those vines grubbed up, to protect the soil about the still growing vines. But that, we knew, was a feeble and short-lasting effort. It was Joseph's turn to find a surer way, to seek for water."

Joseph broke in with all his pleasure in a task that had succeeded.

"We dug six pits along the whole upper bank of the vineyard – if water was found, it was to run down-hill, if we could spare its flowing. Immediately but at substantial depth we found water, living water, flowing and sweet."

"The rock below is limestone, hard and purifying for your streams?" Elisha burst in, hoping to find confirmation here of his long-held theory for watering Israel and he smiled sidelong at Elijah.

"Yes; we had no need to pierce that bedrock but only to hollow out some basins to hold a greater depth of water and to waste none. From these pools which we had now formed below ground, we dug out narrow channels, growing shallower as the land sloped away, and there, when our work on the wells was finished, we had six streams of water, ready to course down the length of the vines to the bottom of the vineyard. We never allowed it to run freely, but dammed it with flat stones, holding it in the depth of the wells until the next evening. We took away these 'gates' each evening, allowing the water to run to the roots in the cool of the day, so that the sun should not steal our labour and the roots have the length of the night to drink their fill."

Naboth had warmed to Joseph's pride in the telling and much of the strain had left his forehead.

"And what of the end of the drought? The vines survived in good heart and you could prune now for a harvest?" Elisha needed a happy outcome to all this labour and Naboth was glad to assure him.

"The very first autumn we gathered bunches. They were not many and the wine we pressed from them had needed a less violent sun. But we had left many clusters on the vines, and here the sun had done its work well. Some of the grapes we gathered, to make the few flasks of rich, sweet wine – which we rarely allow ourselves! – and the rest were raisins, precious in the winter."

"And Joseph's vineyard?" Could the story have a second happy ending?

"You shall see in the first light tomorrow. When we saw, after two years of drought, that we were going to save Naboth's remaining vines, I took cuttings at pruning-time and kept the best to strike as young stock. I planted them in the shade of the older vine-stocks, where the moisture was held as it came from the wells. Soon we saw them bud and with the spring growth we knew that there were ample not only to re-stock my parcel of land but to re-plant those rows of vines which we had sacrificed to Naboth's land. You will see that we have fared well and we have been able to allow the stock which survived the drought to grow one bud higher, giving us alternate rows of high and low vines. It has been a good year for us" – and in the pleasure of his narrative he poured from another vessel.

"Drink it down! It's this year's growth and we have never harvested better!"

As Joseph had promised, the morning saw them abroad in the two vineyards, each showing the successful growth to reward all the care. Elisha, who had never cultivated vines, was loud in his praise.

But the shadow had returned to Naboth's eyes and from the lower reaches of his vineyard he looked up with foreboding to the building of the royal palace which overlooked his ground and with something like fear at the man who came to the balcony, staring down intently at the group below.

By noon, Elijah took Elisha away from Jezreel and made to return towards the towns which bordered Jordan.

King Ahab paced his private chamber, his customary indecision showing in his face and gait. As he looked beyond his palace-wall, he was aware that to the north, where the sight of open country had formerly gladdened him, the dense grove where Jezebel worshipped now closed the way and he had no desire to trespass in those paths. To the south where the fairest valley in his kingdom opened out to the distant plain, the entrance to its streams and thickets was closed below the palace wall by Naboth's vineyard.

From the balcony of his chamber Ahab looked long at this fair acre beneath his walls. There, in orderly rows, extended the vines, pruned and tied to the stakes which marched to the lowest bounds of the orchard. There the vines had been turned and pleached to a hedge, broken only by two gaps which led to the ancient olive trees below. To the left and right, and marking the sloping boundaries of the vineyard, younger olives gave both shelter and an abundant crop. It was as fair a prospect as any Ahab had seen.

And he coveted it. It promised him peace from the affairs of his kingdom. It would counter in his mind the presence of Jezebel's grove and its sordid company. Above all it would be a little kingdom, a paradise in which he could walk along the paths between vines and where, both below in the shade of the olives and above beneath his balcony, he could rest and allow thoughts to fade into silence. Owning it, he would furnish it with arbours, created by almond, peach and nut-trees.

113

Perhaps, if he walked there in the cool of the evening, he would hear other steps and a voice, long silent to his ears, speak of peace, as God the Lord shared his solitude.

So it was the next evening and the next. How could he, with honour, gather this small estate to himself?

On the third morning he put on a rough mantle and went out into the palace-garden. From its shade he entered a path which led to a wicket-gate, rarely used, which opened behind the modest home of Naboth. Walking towards the vineyard, Ahab saw Naboth, resting beneath a fig-tree, where his little garden opened into the vineyard. When Naboth recognised his visitor he stood and invited Ahab to be seated. Ahab waved his invitation aside and broke at once into his plea.

"Naboth, I desire to purchase your vineyard. It shall be more than a just price I shall offer and if that does not please you, I offer you another vineyard, larger and in a fairer place than this, overshadowed as it is by my palace."

Naboth listened with courtesy but his voice was cold as he answered.

"I have no desire, in my advancing years, to leave my customary place. I need no money and no plot of land would be fairer to me than this."

Ahab pleaded like a boy, that in the business of the palace he could never escape the burdens of Israel; that he had nowhere that he could call his own private place where he could walk in peace. Was this vineyard such a boon that a king might ask of his most honoured subject?

Naboth preserved his courtesy and replied with an argument that to any fellow-countryman would have been final:

"This is my family's land, our home for five generations. Most of these olive trees and some of the vines were planted when the parcel of land first came to us.

114

Through the years the blessed seasons and the years of hardship have made this place ever more dear. It is my patrimony! It would be sin to give or sell it, even to you, my king."

Ahab recognised the finality in Naboth's voice and realised that further argument would be demeaning. He returned to the palace, went to his bed-chamber and turned his face to the wall, refusing to take any meal that day.

In late evening Jezebel came to his bed-chamber and asked what sickness kept him from the table and from her company.

"I desired the vineyard of Naboth, for my private leisure, to walk in its shade. But whatever price I offered, the sole reply was a refusal, for it was his valued patrimony, descending from the generations."

The reply was given in a strange desolation, beyond Jezebel's comprehension.

"Are you king in Israel and ruled by the whim of a subject? Leave the outcome to me and trouble yourself no more."

Jezebel gave orders to her chamberlain that he was to summon ten wealthy citizens of Jezreel, outside the circle of Naboth's friends, to wait upon Queen Jezebel in her private chamber at noon the following day.

They assembled as they had been commanded and Jezebel declared her wishes.

"It has come to my ears that Naboth has spoken blasphemy against the gods and treachery against the person of his king. He grows too rampant and must be pruned!"

Though they were no friends of Naboth, they yet knew his integrity; their dealings with him had always been honourable and their disbelief at these charges showed plainly in their silence.

"I would not have you proceed in any unjust way but

115

by full and honourable process of law. Bring him before the assembly of the people, in proper fashion, at the city gate. There the two charges, of blasphemy and treason, may be read in proper form, witnesses called and the truth declared. Go your ways and see it done."

They left reluctantly but had no choice. They took Naboth and imprisoned him and appointed a day when the cause should be heard at the city-gate.

Joseph had seen the flurry of arrest without surprise, for Naboth had told him of Ahab's desire to possess his vineyard. He knew that Naboth's refusal would not end the matter and, knowing that he was powerless to do anything to help him, went with all haste from Jezreel and to Abel-meholah to seek the help of Elijah. He could only pray that he and the prophet would cover the distance from the city before the iniquity was fulfilled.

The day of trial came and Naboth stood before his accusers. Formally they read the brief and unelaborated charges, that Naboth had spoken blasphemy against the gods and treason against the king.

"Since neither time nor place of my supposed iniquities have been laid before you, there is nothing that I can deny. Nor in my past conduct, as all of you can testify, is there the least shadow that would suggest that I am capable of blasphemy or treason. The Lord is the God I love and worship; Ahab is the king, who commands and receives my loyal service."

There was silence as all his accusers knew that he spoke the truth. Then a number of ill-doers, who had been carefully placed among the crowd, began to shout.

"He lies." "We heard him blaspheme the gods and can tell his very words." "He plots the overthrow and the death of Ahab."

The men of substance who constituted the court, knew what had led to this impasse and hated their part in it. They prepared to call a guard to ensure Naboth's safety and at least see him once more imprisoned. But the crowd caught the infection from those who shouted their accusations and when they saw the move to protect Naboth, began a new clamour:

"He is guilty! Stone the blasphemer!" Sufficient hands snatched at Naboth, he was torn from the guard and rushed to open ground outside the city, there to be stoned and his body to lie torn below the walls of Jezreel.

Joseph, Elijah and Elisha arrived at Jezreel some days later. The evil had been done with such haste that some just men had had time to treat Naboth's body with decency and place it in a grave. There Joseph and his friends were taken and there they made their mourning.

Elijah had but one desire before he returned to Abel-meholah with his friends and that was to confront Ahab alone, in his iniquity. He knew that the likeliest place to find him was in Naboth's vineyard, of which he had taken immediate possession. And indeed he found him there, pacing its length, his eyes clouded and his brow dark.

Elijah halted at some distance before him and cried aloud as though addressing a multitude:

> "Thus saith the Lord:
> Hast thou killed and taken possession?
> Thus saith the Lord:
> In the place where dogs licked the blood of Naboth,
> Shall dogs lick thy blood also, even thine."

And Ahab said to Elijah:

> "Hast thou found me, O mine enemy?"

117

and Elijah answered:

> "I have found thee.
> Because thou hast sold thyself,
> To do evil in the sight of the Lord,
> Behold, I will bring evil upon thee,
> And will utterly sweep thee away,
> And will cut off from Ahab
> Every man child.
> Thy house shall be like the house of Jeroboam,
> And like the house of Baasha, son of Ahijah,
> For the provocation wherewith
> Thou hast provoked me to anger
> And hast made Israel to sin."

There was silence between them for Ahab had fallen on his face before Elijah and could make no answer.

> "The dogs shall also devour Jezebel
> By the ramparts of Jezreel
> Him that dieth of Ahab in the city
> The dogs shall eat;
> And him that dieth in the field,
> The fowls in the air shall eat.
> For in thine iniquity,
> There is none like unto thee."

And Ahab tore his garments, put sackcloth on his flesh and fasted, for his iniquities.

And Elijah left him and went his way.

BOOK SEVEN

There was no more to be done at Jezreel; its wrongs had been so great and its pollution had penetrated so deep that only time could heal and purify the city. There would be turmoil and slaughter in the cleansing; Elijah had begun the redeeming history; it was now for God and his other servants to bring the tragedies to their conclusion.

It was clear to Joseph and his friends that there was no place for him now in Jezreel, even if he had wished to stay after the death of Naboth. His own small vineyard could scarcely be a refuge, with Ahab his immediate neighbour and without regret he went down the valley of Jezreel with Elijah and Elisha. He kept the conversation almost wholly concerned with matters of the land: were they now to increase grain-crops, for the greater sustenance of the poor? were they to open more of the land for new fruit crops, the finer citrus fruits and the pomegranates that had been brought from the south and the east? Could one farm carry workers who would grow grain, fruit and vines and at the same time shepherd the hillsides for mutton and wool? At least the questions kept Elisha at full stretch and Elijah, following behind in silence, had time to brood on the future and resolve his mind. He felt that his active life was drawing to its close and the hint on Sinai, that Elisha should

119

succeed him, so far from resolving problems, set more in the forefront of his mind.

Whatever the outcome was to be, Abel-meholah was their first-goal and as they approached the land of Elisha's family, Elijah spoke for the first time for many miles.

"Return to your fields, Elisha and renew your skills. If there is a place for Joseph – and he would be a valuable addition to your family! – take him with you and teach him lowland skills. I shall take my way alone to the wilderness and when the time is right, I shall return and call you once again."

They accepted his judgment and for many weeks, work and leisure matured the friendship of Joseph and Elisha and they knew, whatever the changes of the future, their destinies were now one and inseparable.

For most of these weeks Elijah remained solitary in the wilderness, scarcely breaking his fast and allowing the slow procession of the days to calm – even empty – his mind. When solitude had done its work, he moved to the banks of the Jordan, to a familiar place where a clearing ran down to a pebbly bend in the river, opposite the place where the Brook Kerith emptied its waters into Jordan. Since at no great distance south there was a ford, he knew that no long wait would bring him company. They came: Syrian traders with their bales of merchandise, holy men from lands further east, prophets from Israel who had been to the Syrian desert to know the blessings of solitude. One of these he had known over many years, from the troubled times at Samaria and their first evening's talk had been a sombre regret at the failure of the house of Omri to bring peace to Israel.

"If Ahab had not taken Jezebel to wife, would our history have been different and happier?"

"A vain question! All is in God's hands and we wait simply on his will."

They remained together for some days and Elijah caught at the repeated hints in his companion's conversation that new prophecy was kindling the young men of Israel. Elijah too had sensed a change – there had been shadows of this new power in the words of Elisha – but had been too occupied with his own concerns to give it much thought.

"They gather in small schools of prophecy. They make no show of learning, for most of them are simple toilers on the land; but when they gather for the evening worship, their ecstacy before the Lord is as the singing of heaven's hosts descended to earth!"

Elijah listened in some amazement. The company of other prophets had never been his way – he sought none and was rarely sought by them. But what of Elisha and Joseph? and what was to be his part in their vocation?

He returned to Abel-meholah and found the two young men ready for anything that lay before them. Elijah immediately questioned Elisha about the presence in their neighbourhood of prophet-bands.

"Yes; not great. Six or seven young men, brothers and cousins from farms below us here, on the way to Gilgal. They are simple people, like myself. They have no skills but those of the mattock and plough but they have listened with care and love to the words of Torah and they tell me that they have heard the voice behind Torah, the voice 'that speaks in the ancient places' – that is how they describe it. I went with them one evening to a quiet place in the hills above Gilgal and there I listened with joy. One of them recited the psalms of David and another – a darker voice – repeated the early words of the Law as we received it from the mouth of Moses. Indeed, for a moment, in that half-light, it seemed to me that Moses himself was there, speaking in the quiet tones of that young voice.

"But that was not all. There was silence after those words of his and then another began to sing. The notes were quiet, scarcely more than a breath on the air, and the melody was one I had never heard before. And yet it had hints of a shepherd-song and I knew why the psalms were so dear to them.

"The melody appeared to be drawing to its end but then another voice took it up, at a lower pitch and the two voices mingled in harmony. Then there was a third – and a fourth – and all were singing together and even I was caught in the harmony. I knew then what they meant when they told me of 'ecstacy.' Their eyes shone and these simple men were taken beyond themselves, speaking and singing words which were echoes of the heroes, of the holiness of ancient times."

Elijah knew that the answer to his brooding was there, in the words of Elisha.

"We are a people of history, of heroes and mighty deeds. We have a past, but have we a present, a future? These young men have found a truth, in joy to revel in the words and deeds of old time. Call them, Elisha, invite them to a journey with us. Perhaps a new truth may be given us."

They went south to the rich lands west of Jordan and there they joined the small group of young countrymen. They were glad and perhaps a little awed, to meet Elijah, for truth had already been enlarged to legend in the accounts that had reached them of all that he had done. He spoke little with them but said he hoped they would accompany him to Gilgal.

When they reached the northern outskirts Elijah paused at a height above the town and said to them.

"We have returned to the beginning. This is where history began for this land. There to the east is Jordan, first crossed by Joshua and this place is the first fragment of the promise to Moses. And here Joshua commanded that twelve stones be raised as a memorial, that here the twelve tribes of our nation first crossed to their new home."

The little group was silent and Joseph, the stranger to these parts of their country, looked with a mingled awe and anticipation for the commands that must surely issue from these words.

"But men are perverse, even we of God's chosen! The people of Israel demanded a king that should give them power like their neighbours. And here in Gilgal Saul was crowned and you know his history."

These young men had been hardened by their work but made sensitive by their prophetic calling; with Joshua and Saul at the front of their minds, they prepared there for their night's rest. But first, Joseph and Elijah were to hear the descent of ecstacy. Psalm, Torah, the chant – it swept them into its rhythm, and as it died away they went to their rest in a great peace.

The following morning Elijah told them that Bethel was to be their next goal. It was a hard day's journey through the hill country and again as they reached the city outskirts, Elijah halted them.

"Bethel, a place of noble memory! You will never forget that here the heavens opened – the heavens do open, my sons! – and here in his weariness, Jacob lay down to his rest, expecting nothing. And yet the vision came. From heaven to earth a stream of light and an ascent like the steps to a high temple. And to the vision was added the harmony of heaven as the angels of God descended and ascended, their several melodies uniting in the glorious harmony of their Lord God. But why do I remind you of this? Beyond all my knowledge of the ways of the Lord, you have heard that harmony and respect it in your song. Gilgal saw the beginning of the journey, Bethel its heavenly confirmation. I have brought you here today that you may strengthen your resolve. My sole prophet's vision now is this: With Elisha, my eldest son in the will of God, you will go out in your strength to renew the vision of Israel, to sing Israel's melodies and to purify her way.

"Now you will come with me to Jordan and wait on its bank, while I cross to find once more the will of God. I know that my time with you is short but I have faith in the purity of your strength."

They made their way past Jericho until they reached the bank of Jordan and as Elijah prepared to cross, Elisha eagerly begged that he might come with him.

"It is my end, Elisha. I go to the presense of the Lord our God, awaiting his judgment. You have no place there, at the entrance to my end on earth."

"I am your son and if this is to be the end, I claim, as of inheritance, the double portion of an eldest son, a double portion of your power and spirit of prophecy."

"If indeed you see me at my taking away, then this inheritance will be yours."

The band of young men waited on the shore and saw Elijah remove his cloak, fold it together and strike with it at the waters of Jordan. They parted and the two prophets crossed to the other bank on dry land.

There Elijah stood and looked to the heavens while Elisha fell to his knees and tried to pray. From a cloudless sky came a single shaft of lightning which struck the ground between them. Then without sound, but like the sight of a tempest on Sinai, the lightning shafts followed swiftly, circling Elijah with their fire. As Elisha cowered before this silent storm, there came a rushing sound as of winds and mighty waters, and through the encircling shafts of lightning a massive chariot of fire descended, the flame of the horses' manes reaching out beyond the lightning shafts.

Elijah was swept into the heart of the flame and as the chariot flew upwards, so the lightning ceased and there was greater peace than before the vision.

There, where the chariot had descended, was the mantle of Elijah. The young man humbly placed it over his shoulders and walked with a new resolution towards Jordan. On the opposite bank the little band of prophets waited his return and wondered at the absence of Elijah. Elisha stood before them, removed the mantle and folded it, and with Elijah's gesture, struck the waters. They parted, granting him a ford of dry ground.

Elisha had inherited the portion of the eldest son.

JESHUA
Moelwyn Merchant

'His is a gripping narrative which maintains the pace and tension of the gospel story, and yet places it within a context of dialogue and action convincing to our own age. It's reverent, but not sentimental, and religious without being milk-and-water; robustly pious and penetrating in its insights.' Prof. Glanmor Williams, *Western Mail*

'This is a long novel: reverent, profound, yet homely and natural, testifying to that truth. For believers it succeeds before it starts; for the uncommitted with open eyes and receptive hearts it may yet open doors.' *The Church Times*

0 7154 0684 1   £10.95